SA

SATAN!

SATAN!

a

Tony White

novel

First published in 1999 by ATTACK! Books
83 Clerkenwell Road, London EC1 5AR
Copyright: Tony White 1999
Layout by Rom
Original artwork by Paul McAffery
Printed and bound in Great Britain by
Woolnough Book Binding Ltd
Irthlingborough, North Hants

SATAN! SATAN! SATAN! is a work of avant-pulp fiction. Any
similarities between characters in this book and real people, alive
or dead, is entirely coincidental.

WARNING! Reading ATTACK! books in an enclosed space can
result in violent epileptic fits involving much thrashing, writhing and
foaming at the mouth and - in extreme cases - attempts to chew
off one's own face. If in any doubt, please consult a doctor before
continuing.

ALSO AVALIABLE FROM ATTACK!

TITS-OUT TEENAGE TERROR TOTTY by Steven Wells
RAIDERS OF THE LOW FOREHEAD by Stanley Manly

ATTACK! is an imprint of Creation Books.

Thanks to whoever it was that circulated the 1984 transcript of Jim Jones's suicide speech (which is used in its entirety throughout chapter 20).

Big thanks also go out to Sarah Such, the Butthole Surfers, Davey Notarius, Swells and Stewart Home.

VIVA ATTACK!

Disgruntled ex-postal worker Tony White is the author of the crustie cult classic *Road Rage!* and the cop/alien abduction masterpiece *charlieunclenorfolktango*.

He also edited the best selling *britpulp!* anthology.

Tony lives in London's notorious Whitechapel district and is a well known "face" on the capital's white wine'n'teckno avant-pulp literary circuit.

I

Someone had sprayed an inverted cross on the wall. And a whole host of grinning skulls, dripping with red paint, that seemed to mock the three girls who knelt on the cold concrete floor beneath it as if they were taking part in some sacreligious benediction. And in a way they were. Deb reached inside her leather jacket, taking out a small paper package which she carefully unfolded. The music outside was reduced to a distant, muffled bass-line but the friends still recognised the howling intro to the latest Dogs of Thor single and exchanged knowing looks as Deb - pausing only to wipe away a stray pube - gently tapped the paper wrap and sprinkled some of the powder onto the lid.

'It's pink, Deb.'

'Yeah I know. Jez says the pink stuff's the best though.'

Tish cackled:

'Well 'e should know. That fucker's shoved more grammes up iz nose than the whole of fucking Leeds put together! Come on Deb, line 'em up then.'

Deb pulled out the razor blade that hung around her neck and began cutting the speed to get rid of the lumps. Then, with a couple of deft swipes, she produced three perfect lines.

'Oh shit I 'aven't got any notes.'

'Me neither. Fuck it.'

'Ang on a sec,' said Tish rummaging in her pockets, 'Ah, here it is.'

She pulled out a flyer for an up-coming gig and began to roll it up.

'S'about fuckin' time this lot did summat useful.'

'Aye,' Deb agreed. 'Mind you, that Richie's alright - 'E said we could get in for nowt.....'

'Yeah, he would! The dirty bastard!'

The girls took turns to bend low over the bog lid and snort up the speed. Seconds later they crashed out of the cubicle into the brightly lit bogs, then over to the mirror to make some final adjustments. They looked like walking corpses with their white faces, their black lips and them big black shadows round their eyes. Tish was the tallest of the three, the biggest and all, and her long black hair was back-combed into gravity-defying heights. She tended to pull skinny small blokes who wanted to be smothered by her massive tits. Sal and Deb were both skinny as they come. Sal had shaved the sides of her head and the resulting black mohican was crimped to fuck. Deb's hair hung lank and lifeless to her shoulders. With their tattoos and ripped-up fishnets, their victorian whale bone corsets and their junkshop Whitby Jet jewellery they looked totally fucking wicked.

As they pushed their way out of the bogs and into the crowded club someone shouted:

'Ey, it's the three fuckin' witches. Alright girls?'

'Yeah,' Tish cackled again. 'But fuckin' watch out, Bilko, or I'll cast a fuckin' spell on yer.'

'Gonna turn me into a fuckin' frog are yer?'

'Don't need to you ugly fucker, you look like a fuckin' frog already.'

'Need any gear, girls?'

'No ta!' they chorused as one – their laughter disappearing into the crowd with them.

Bilko was well known as the purveyor of bad quality drugs which he always cut to fuck soze he'd have more for izself. Striking in appearance, with his broken nose and the bulbous eyes which appeared even more bug-like behind the thick black-framed glasses which assumed permanent residence on his face, and rarely if ever seen without a can of ULTRA STRONG LAGER™ in his hand, Bilko could be a bit of a laff when he wasn't nodding out on the after effects of whatever shit he'd been stickin' in his arm, but since that didn't happen very often not many people knew it. Debs always thought of him as a bit of a clown and chose to forget the one time she'd bought gear off him and felt like death-warmed-up for a week. Once you knew that though, and never to buy his 'money up front and I'll just go and get the stuff for yer' spiel – a guarantee you'd not see him for fucking weeks – he was harmless enough. But Bilko was not part of the plan for this or any other night out.

The Hell-fire club was pumping: this was gonna be a fucking good one. For a change the place was full of horny-looking goth blokes - rather than the usual range of university boys who only acted like decadent faggots cos they were crap in bed - and Debs was hoping that there'd be at least one who was man enough to jump at the chance of taking the three of them on at once. She had her eye on one in particular. A new face she'd not seen before. He'd been standing by the door when they'd come in. He looked effete, almost feminine, with the barest hint of black kohl around his blood-shot eyes. And, unlike everyone else in the club, he had blonde hair, which was cut into a neat and timeless style. He'd been looking at the floor, avoiding eye contact with the punters he was handing flyers too. Despite this apparent gentleness though there was something odd about him, something that made him seem ultimately cor-ruptible, something that made her blood run cold and her cunt red-hot. Just thinking about him now set her quiveringly afire.

'You know where I am, girls,' Bilko shouted after them, slightly embarassed. But no-one was listening, and Bilko realised that for a change it was him, not his drugs, that had been cut. He took a swig of ULTRA STRONG LAGER™, tapped his pocket for the reassuring rattle of his works and shouldered his way through the throng.

The bogs stank to high heaven. Here and there aban-doned club flyers soaked up the beer and piss and a steady drip of water from somewhere had formed weird concrete stalactites on the ceiling. Bilko took the speed out of his pocket and did a bit of quick mental arithmetic. He'd planned to sell two wraps to fund his evening's beer and save the other for him and Debs to snort later, a trump card to pull out of his pocket and wave in her face when she was really lagging. But that prospect was looking pretty remote, not only had she barely noticed him, it looked like Jez had beaten him to it with the supplies. The bastard. Fuck it, he thought, do the lot and ponce a beer off Ron when I come down off the fucking ceiling.

*

When the lights came on several hours later Tish, Sal and Deb were speeding out of their fucking heads and giggling like a bunch of satanic school-girls. It had been an evil night. There were a couple of Japanese goths dominating the dance floor with their eerie clockwork robotics, while everyone else stood around looking sombre with their pints of guinness or lager and black. Well almost everyone; it seemed like everywhere she'd looked there was Bilko, dashing around like a demented fucking ferret and yammering at anyone who'd listen, looking even more bug-eyed than usual, and all the while looking over his shoulder and trying to catch her eye. It was obvious that he was trying to impress her but the thought of fucking Bilko... well it just didn't bear thinking about at all.

Deb had spent most of the night trying to avoid him, trying to find the weird guy who'd been standing by the door but he'd seemed to have vanished into thin air. She'd asked a couple of former fucks if they knew who he was, but they just looked at her strangely and said nothing. For fuck's sake, just cos she didn't wanna fuck them any more was no reason for them to get all jealous now. Finally, in desperation, the three of them had hooked up with a cool bunch of blokes with tattoos and pony-tails who said they were roadies on the last Sisters of Mercy tour and had bottles of Jack Daniels in the inside pockets of their ancient leather jackets. For some reason these guys seemed to have found them really amusing, she'd caught them exchanging wry smiles with each other while they regaled them with hilarious back stage stories about Eldritch and the others. They'd even been on tour with Bauhaus, and it'd been really spooky cos just as Pete started telling them about it the DJ'd put on Bela Lugosi's Dead. A right fucking coincidence.

'Talk of the devil!', Tish cackled. They'd all pissed themselves laughing.

It took more than a few sips of Jack Daniels to get inside Deb's knickers but the when the three of them disappeared to the bogs and hoovered up the last of Jez's speed, Tish had just said, 'Fuck it, Andy's got great tats, I wonder if his nipples are pierced' and that was that. When the music was turned down and the guys had invited them on to a party ('I think some of the Sisters might be there...') Deb knew that for a start they'd be the only ones going, that it'd just be the six of them in some shit bedsit, and that these guys were just after fucking some star-struck goth chicks, but she didn't care:

'Yeah, sound. We'd love to.'

And maybe, just maybe, some of the Sisters really would be there.

On the way out of the club Pete had pointed out a sleeping bundle curled up in one of the booths.

'Look at that cunt!'

'Eh, it's fucking Bilko,' said Tish.

Sal cackled:

'Twat must've been tekkin his own stuff!'

With that they all roared with laughter and pushed their way through the doors to the exit. As they did so, Deb caught sight of a stack of flyers set on the floor where the mysteriously attractive blonde boy had been standing. She picked one off the top of the pile and stuffed it into Sal's handbag.

It was warm outside and Tish announced that she was feeling really devil-may-care.

'Where's this fucking party then, Andy?'

'Woodhouse.'

'Let's tek a fucking detour.'

'Sound.'

A few minutes later they were squeezing through a gap

in the ancient iron railings that surrounded the ruined church near Woodhouse Moor. A couple of late buses went past but apart from that no-one had seen them going in. The streets were dead except for some distant laughter and the occasional drunken scream. There was a full moon which helped them pick their way through the ivy and brambles which tangled around the ruined statuary. Headless angels stood guard as they sat down on the damp grass behind a big tomb. One side of it was caved in and they all peered in with a cigarette lighter, but all they could see was the bricks. There was no body. Dave took his bottle out and they passed it around, the whiskey burning their throats, numbing their lips, but doing little to counteract the speed which coursed through their veins.

'I'll skin up then,' said Andy.

'Wicked,' said Sal. 'What've you got?'

'Black.'

'Sound!'

Andy got some skins out of his pocket and began to stick them together in the time-honoured fashion. Then he nicked one of Pete's Marlboroughs and began to roll a joint. Minutes later he was striking a lucifer which he flicked into the night once it had done its job. After blowing out the flame which bloomed momentarily on the end of the spliff, he drew the powerful smoke deep into his lungs.

They'd all paired up then. In the graveyard. One or two bats were flying erratically around above their heads, snapping up the last of the midges, and when the moon disappeared behind an ancient yew the darkness had lent some intimacy to the proceedings. Deb found herself on her feet.

'Come on then.'

She grabbed the nearest bottle with one hand and took a swig, then pointed it at Pete who scrambled to his feet. He necked it, took a sharp intake of breath through his teeth, then wiped the back of his hand across his lips and expressed his satisfaction. Then he got a flash of stocking as Deb lifted her skirt to step over a grave and hurried after her.

'Hang on.'

They found a flat gravestone that was clear of brambles and ivy. They kissed long and deep. The elaborately curlicued script that had once announced the name of he who rotted beneath them was too worn to read, but while they kissed Deb felt Pete's hands pushing up beneath the torn black silk of her bodice, felt him tracing some equally elaborate sentiments on her skin with his finger tips and this message was clear enough.

Deb reached down to knead his cock which was beginning to strain against his black levis. Pete took a sharp intake of breath through his teeth before expressing his satisfaction. Then he slipped his hand down the front of her dress and began to caress her tits. When he lightly pinched one of her nipples it seemed to flick a switch in her cunt and she suddenly squirmed with the instant heat of her devilish desires. Deb lifted up her skirt and grabbed his hand out of her top, placing it on the smooth skin of her thigh, Pete didn't need any further encouragement and his fingertips snaked up around her knickers, pulling them to one side in his eagerness to find the bitch's hot hell hole. He quickly pushed through the thick pubes that crowded around her cunt, then parted her quivering lips, pinching and pulling at her clit with a demonic glint in his eye. Deb reacted like a creature possessed, she sank her teeth into his neck and sucked till she could taste the bruise, while her other hand wrestled with his belt and flies to liberate his blood-filled love bone from the bounds of decency.

'Suck my cock!' he pleaded.

'Bugger that!' said Deb as she put a hand on his chest and pushed him roughly down onto the cold stone. She gathered up her skirts about her with one hand and straddled him then grabbed his cock and guided it to the hairy gates of hades.

'I wanna ride you to hell and back you randy bastard!' she shouted as she impaled herself on his enormous, veiny cock and, as if in reply, he drove it unerringly into the hot, pulsating heart of her being. Pete felt the walls of the underworld closing in on him as Deb bucked and howled above him like a banshee bitch on heat. As they both came the sights and sounds of the night-time graveyard melted away, only to be replaced by a Bosch-like landscape of decadent and twisted desire; an empire of ungodly gratification. Deb and Pete had created a Garden of Earthly Delights and, as he shot what seemed like gallons of hot spunk into her convulsing cunt, they saw that it was good.

II

'For thy seed shall be as asses milk, and thy seed shall be in many waters, and it shall cleanse them that drink thereof, and his king shall be higher than agag, and his kingdom shall be exalted. But heed my words. Let not thine enemies drink of thy goodness: they shall be smitten before thy face, they shall come out against thee one way, and flee before thee seven ways...'

The White Welshman paused in his thunderous oration, placing his hand on the altar to steady himself. He took a deep breath and felt the holy spirit filling his body with light, anointing him with the power of God. As he exhaled he felt minute particles of the holy ghost leaving his body, mingled with his very breath. He fought the impulse to close his mouth, to breathe through his nose in order to minimise the loss, then laughed inwardly at his vanity and raised his eyes to heaven, muttering a silent prayer of thanks for the privilege of being such a perfect vessel. His eyes filled with tears of joy.

'Thank you lord for filling us with thy spirit!' he thundered.

'Amen!' came the automatic response from the assembled members of the Church of the Everlasting Day.

The albino preacher looked around at his church, and he saw that it was good. Surveying the flock who knelt at his feet, Jeremiah Jones took another deep breath and quite deliberately exhaled in their direction. After all there was enough of the holy spirit to go around. Yeah, he thought to himself, the lord hath truly filled my cup! And was it not the case that on those cold and distant mornings on the shores of Gallilee that people did raise their vestments when they spake to the Lord in an attempt to absorb some of His foggy morning breath? Yeah, verily it was true. And did he smite them down? No, he did not. There was enough of the holy spirit to go around. And did they not gather up the steaming fruits of His body and venerate them, building churches where He had strained and squatted in the wilderness? They surely did. Jones benignly surveyed the blonde heads bowed in prayer around him.

'Let him who believeth receive the word of the Lord!'

'Amen!' chorused the acolytes of the Welshman.

'Let him who believeth allow the humble servant of the Lord to cleanse him in his name!'

'Amen!' chorused the disciples once again.

'And who among ye is most deserving of that most noble duty which our Lord hath set down in the scriptures so that we might be cleansed, the better to receive the word of God in our hearts?'

As the flock clamoured at his feet, kissing his robes in supplication, he felt the hand of the Lord settling on his loins. It was time. He gave over his body to God. I am but a puppet of Your will, he mouthed in silent prayer, show me the way. Show me who here is worthy to do your work.

A shaft of sunlight suddenly shone through the stained glass window behind the altar, illuminating the motes of dust which swirled above them and alighting on the head of one who did not clamour on all fours, singling out the one who still knelt in silent prayer. The meek, thought Jeremiah, shall truly inherit the earth.

'Thank you Lord,' he thundered. 'For showing thy humble servant the way!'

'Amen!' mumbled the blessed flock, their mouths buried in his vestments as they clutched his hems in devout and willing servitude.

Jeremiah Jones stepped forward, scattering his minions like so many autumn leaves, and lay his hand down on the head of she who would serve the Lord.

'Come, young lady. The Lord hath spoken.'

The devout supplicant began to scramble to her feet, then looked up at Jones's pure white face as the sunlight formed a halo around his snowy mass of hair. She met the quizzical expression that flickered across the albino brow of Jeremiah

Jones; saw the error of her ways reflected in that holy, pink eyed gaze; felt the steady pressure of the hand which rested, not so lightly now, upon her head. She fell forward onto her hands and crawled up the steps like the dirty bitch that she undoubtedly was in the eyes of the Lord.

Jones took the chalice from the altar and, taking care not to spill the holy water with which it was filled, he held it up and made the sign of the cross, blessed it in the eyes of the Lord, then clutched it to his chest.

'The Lord thy God hath shown me that the holy river Jordan is within us,' thundered Jerremiah Jones.

'Amen!'

'And you, girl,' murmered Jones as he tucked a finger under the comely acolyte's chin and forced her head up to heed the word of God, 'Is there one among these many waters that thou hast given of today?'

Shamefacedly the disciple shook her head.

'And from the south give up, saith the Lord, and from the west keep not back, ye cannot hold back the waters of the holy Jordan river,' his voice hushed to a near whisper of entreaty. 'Are you worthy to let your waters flow in the eyes of the Lord thy God?'

She nodded, raising her simple cotton tunic as the melanin-deficient minister placed the golden chalice on the floor in front of her. It was almost full, but she squatted above it and let loose her waters as commanded. The amber fluid within the goblet overflowed, and the colourless cleric licked his lips in delight. When the flood had abated he picked up the chalice and held it to his breast, raising his eyes to heaven and mouthing a silent prayer of thanks.

The girl fumbled with the Welshman's vestments, quickly finding what she was looking for. In a trice she had liberated the pale preacher's pure white prick from beneath his purple robes.

As the attractive acolyte gave him a righteous hand job, Jones saw the way, the truth and the light and felt the holy spirit trembling in his loins.

'This is my body!' he thundered. 'Eat it! That ye might enter the kingdom of heaven!'

As the supplicant sucked on the staff of life, Jeremiah knew that the word of God would surely burst forth. He whacked her on the side of the head, then handed down the jewelled chalice. He took a sharp intake of breath through his teeth before loudly expressing his satisfaction.

'Thank you Lord! My cup brimmeth over!' he exploded, as the hot host spurted into the holy waters.

'For thy seed shall be as asses milk, and thy seed shall be in many waters, and it shall cleanse them that drink thereof,' he intoned as the chalice was passed among the devout that they might sip the blessed liquid within. 'And yeah his king shall be higher than agag, and his kingdom shall be exalted. But heed my words. Let not thine enemies drink of thy goodness: they shall be smitten before thy face, they shall come out against thee one way, and flee before thee seven ways...'

III

It was late afternoon before Deb crawled out of bed. By the time they'd left the graveyard it was almost dawn, and Jez's whizz had well and truly worn off. Dave, Pete and Andy had staggered off home and all, but not before getting the phone numbers which seemed to guarantee further fornication with the horny black-garbed goth birds.

Sal and Tish were still asleep. They'd all been so knackered when they got back that they hadn't had time to compare notes on the night's conquests.

Deb put the kettle on and turned on the radio. Then, as a hit of the day blasted out, she thought better of it and quickly slapped it off again. Fuck it, she felt rough. She'd slept through the come down off the speed, but now the hangover from everything else was starting to kick in. Her legs ached and for some reason her knees hurt. Then as she examined the grazes on both knees she remembered fucking Pete. On a fucking gravestone! A police car sped past with its siren blaring, but Deb barely noticed it, so wrapped up was she in the events of the previous night. She smiled to herself as she poured the water into her cup, laughing out loud as she dropped the tea bag into the overflowing black bin liner that sat in the corner of the kitchen, carefully averting her eyes from the cartons of rotting milk and festering muck within. In the next room Tish groaned as she stirred into something approaching wakefulness. Deb reached up and grabbed another mug off the shelf.

*

In a basement flat further down the hill Bilko woke with a start. A police car had sped past with its siren blaring and the sudden noise jarred into some bizarre dream in which Bilko had indeed been turned into a frog and was hopping forlornly around the linoleum corridors of the Department of Social Satisfaction office trying to sort out his claim. It was with some relief then that he returned to the land of the living. He'd been lying face down on the bed, fully clothed, hadn't even taken off his donkey jacket. As he swung his feet off the bed and tried to sit up, a wave of intense nausea washed over him, his mouth suddenly filling with the bitter contents of his stomach and a cold sweat drenching his face. He managed to run to the bog before his body rejected, with some violence, the semi-digested kebab and chips and the ULTRA STRONG LAGER™ which it found so offensive.

When his body returned to some kind of delicate equilibrium, and he weakly groped his way back into the bedsit he was surprised to see a spade leaning against the chair. A garden spade. Well, probably a shovel. 'L.C.C.' announced the initials which were burnt into the wood. Then he caught sight of the dirty Morrisons carrier bag which, judging from it's position on the bed, he'd been snuggled up to all night. At that moment he suddenly remembered a little of the night before, and what he had done after the bouncers had so rudely chucked him out of the empty club. Then his stomach convulsed and, clamping a dirty hand across his mouth to stem the flow, he ran back out of the room and knelt at the bog while his violated gut finished the job it had started a few minutes before.

*

Tish had surfaced now too. The three goth birds sat supping tea at the kitchen table. No-one was talking and eye make up was smeared down their faces. Every now and then one or other of them would put their head in their hands and groan loudly.

'Eh Deb,' said Tish finally. 'Have you got any fucking paracetamol or what?'

Without replying, Deb stood up and rummaged in a drawer, pulling out a bottle of painkillers and a long forgotten packet of Black Sobranie left over from some other night out. She struggled with the top of the paracetamol bottle and then dispensed a couple of tablets each to her friends.

'Oh good!' said Sal, stuffing them in her gob and taking a swig of tea. 'Breakfast!'

'Dinner more like!' said Tish, necking hers.

'No. S'fuckin supper, innit!' corrected Sal, looking out the window at the rapidly progressing day. Well, fuck it, the day could progress without them. They were creatures of the fucking night weren't they, eh?

Deb took one of the timelessly decadent cigarettes from the packet and then inquisitively shook a packet of greasy lucifers that had been sat on the filthy table for the past few months. Opening it up she impatiently discarded a few sticks of useless charcoal before finding one which hadn't yet been used. Striking it, she took a deep and slightly ostentatious drag on the stale Sobranie then shook the acrid-smelling lucifer out and replaced it in the box.

*

Down the hill Bilko was sitting at the table of his flat. He'd been out to the shops to fetch his breakfast and a few other bits and bobs and was now supping from a cold tin of ULTRA STRONG LAGER™. He'd put the latest record by The Dogs of Thor on the turntable and was tapping his foot as he listened to the howling guitars of the satanic Swedish songsters. He put down his lager for a sec and took out his Old Holborn. Opening up the plastic pack he dug around amongst the moist and finely shredded contents, eventually digging out a packet of orange Rizlas. Moments later he was striking an acrid-smelling lucifer and taking a long drag on a tatty roll-up, drawing the fragrant smoke deep into his lungs, pausing only to spit out a stray piece of tobacco.

At last he was starting to feel vaguely human again. Which was more than he could say for a certain someone, thought Bilko with a self-satisfied snigger. The revulsion he'd felt on waking had now receded, to be replaced by an unshakeable sense of what a clever bastard he really was. He wasn't very good on cleaning products though. Hadn't ever seen the need for them before, and certainly hadn't realised how many different ones there were. So much fucking choice. Who bought this shit for fuck's sake? He couldn't work out whether Jif would be better than Domestos or if Flash was more efficient than Harpic. Who could fucking tell. Sparkling whiteness wasn't really his thing and none of the bottles had any instructions for the job he'd in mind for it. Couldn't really ask either could he, eh? The thought of it had made him laugh out loud in the shop, just imagining the expression on the dopy shop assistant's face when he realised what kind of man he was dealing with here: 'Excuse me mate, v'you got anything for...' He'd looked up in mid-guffaw and caught sight of the cashier surveying him via the curved surface of the anti-shoplifting mirror. Pull yourself together, son he'd thought, then straightened up, cleared his throat and tried to look like a normal shopper. In the end he'd just bought all of them. The guy behind the counter had looked at him quizzically. All Bilko'd ever been in for before was his daily supply of ULTRA STRONG LAGER™.

'Spring cleaning is it then?' he'd asked.

'Yeah, thassit, yeah. Tidying up, mate !' Bilko'd confirmed, barely managing to supress a slightly hysterical giggle. When he'd got home he'd just tipped the lot into the bath and left the various brightly coloured fluids to get on with it.

*

It was about then that Deb found the flyer. It was printed all in black and red, not like the day-glo smiley faces that appealed to the run-of-the-mill clubber.

'Eh, look at this girls...' she'd said, tossing it onto the table in front of her mates.

Written in gothic script across the top was the legend:

the festival of night

Then beneath that:

whitby abbey 31st october

That was fucking Halloween. Sound.

'Eh, wicked! Less fuckin' go then.' enthused Sal, echoing Deb's thoughts exactly. 'How much is it?'

'Fuck, it's thirty fuckin quid.'

'Who's playin then?' asked Tish, slightly slow off the mark.

Sal read the list of bands aloud:

'Dogs of Thor, Succubus, Hell Whores, Christian Cock Suckers, Sisters, Bauhaus, Sepultura, Cubanate, 'the Neph'', Roses of Avalanche, The Australian Whitehouse, The Australian Mayhem...'

'Oh ace, I'll not be missin that!' Tish shouted, barely able to contain her excitement. She reached for the Black Sobranie and struck an acrid-smelling lucifer before drawing the smoke deep into her lungs. 'Thass fuckin' sound is that. Eh, d'you reckon the lads'll be able to gerrus in?'

Oh yeah! thought Deb. The fucking Sisters were playing. Pete'd probably be able to get her in for nowt.

'Well they might need a bit of persuading!' she cackled. 'But I'm sure they'll see sense!'

*

Bilko had drained the bath, and now a pan was bubbling away on the burner. This'd definitely impress Deb. She'd not be able to resist him. He'd been listening to The Dogs of Thor all afternoon, but now he'd got the telly on, just for a bit of background. He went into the kitchen and peered into the pan. This was boiling up a treat. The steam misted up his milk-bottle-bottom glasses, and the disinfectant in the water stung his eyes a little. Give it an hour, he thought. He went to the fridge and pulled out another can of ULTRA STRONG LAGER™, cracking it open as he went back into his room. He surveyed the shabby furniture that came with the flat. He'd been a bit shocked while flicking through the photos in a pal's true crime book a couple of months before to realise that he had the same carpet as Dennis fucking Neilson. The mass murderer. Boiled up bodies and shit. He wondered for a second if the carpet itself could be evil, if there was something about the design that fucked with people's heads, then caught himself, thought better of it, necked some lager and went and sat down in the tatty armchair. Placing his beer on one arm he looked around for his Old Holborn, finally rummaging down the side of the cushion. A few moments later he was striking an acrid-smelling lucifer and drawing the fragrant smoke deep into his lungs. The news-reader on the telly interrupted his reverie:

'And the headlines tonight. Breakaway Loyalist terror groups objecting to the Good Friday Peace Agreement in Northern Ireland have claimed responsibility for the 2,000 lb bomb which this afternoon exploded in Belfast's Roman Catholic Cathedral, killing 23 people. Police and Security Forces are unsure how a bomb a bomb of this size could have been planted beneath the building, which is a focal point for worship among Catholics all over the Province. Over now to our Northern Ireland correspondent Seamus O'Connor in Belfast. Seamus, what could be going through the minds of...'

Bilko's limited attention span gave out at the possibility of some boring old suit's rigorous analysis. Preferring to look at the scene behind the veteran news reporter, he watched as the once impressive building was reduced to little more than a flam-ing wreck. Suddenly the spire gave a great shudder and collapsed into the inferno within. It looked totally fucking sound. Like sommat from a film. Like from The Omen or sommat. He supped again at his ULTRA STRONG LAGER™ and took an experimental puff at his cigarette. Nothing. He'd been so engrossed in the news that the roll-up had gone out, but picking up the box of lucifers it was only a matter of seconds before he got it going again.

By the time he looked up at the telly again the story had moved on:

'And The Bishop of Derby has today caused controversy among Church of England Leaders by claiming that Judas, and not Jesus Christ, was truly the Son of God. He has said that his comments were taken out of context. A spokesman for the General Synod has however refused to issue a statement, saying only that in light of todays horrific events in Northern Ireland it would be inappropriate to focus on the minutiae of theological debate, and that the sympathy and the thoughts of church-goers everywhere should surely be with the people of Northern Ireland in this tragic hour...'

Bilko switched the telly's sound off in disgust, they'd hardly showed it at all. They probably had loads of film of the fucking church burning down and all they could go on about was some religious ponce in fucking Derby. He pressed play then banged out an imaginary chord as the howling guitar intro to the title track of the new Dogs of Thor album kicked in. Moments later a discordant bass pumped up the volume before Vlad Vargstrom's demonic vocal began to shriek across the desolate landscape of sound, conjuring up the image of angry and vengeful Norse gods racing like supernatural wolves across a primitive Europe and extinguishing the flames of hope. Pushing his glasses back up his nose, Bilko joined in with Vargstrom's stream of vicious vocal invective:

>Sacreligious, SACK religious, he shouted,
>Mind and body, We are one.
>Sacreligious, SACK religious,
>Bird air sinking churches daaaaaaaaaaaaaaaagh!

Bilko punched the air as the howling guitar crashed into life once more.

>We reclaim what's ours by right,
>We are coming in the night,
>Rape and murder are our creed,
>Kill the bitches, watch them BLEEEEEED!

Then he jumped around the room as the chorus kicked in for the last time. This song was a two minute blitzkreig from the darker side of the Scandinavian imagination and he fucking loved it. Vargstrom sounded like a demented old witch getting fucked up the arse by the devil himself.

> 𝕾acreligious, 𝕾𝕬𝕮𝕶 religious,
> 𝕸ind and body, 𝖂e are one.
> 𝕾acreligious, 𝕾𝕬𝕮𝕶 religious,
> 𝕭ird air sinking churches daaaaaaaaaaaaaaaagh!
> 𝕭ird air sinking churches daaaaaaaaaaaaaaaagh!

But something wasn't right. 'Bird air sinking churches daaaagh?' The more he sang along with the brutal sounding nonsense poem, the more nonsensical it became. Suddenly the image of the bombed cathedral flashed onto the screen for the closing headlines and Bilko realised the truth of what Vargstrom was urging:

𝕭urn their stinking churches down!
𝕭urn their stinking churches down!
𝕭urn their stinking churches down!
𝕭urn their stinking churches down!

Strangely ennervated by this revelation, Bilko put the track back to the beginning then went out into the kitchen to check the pan, taking an experimental drag at his roll-up on the way. It had gone fucking out again. He lit it from the stove, then turned off the gas. It must be done by now. Pulling down his sleeves he put an ill-fitting lid on the saucepan, then, fag in mouth, his eyes watering from the smoke, he poured the dirty water and disinfectant down the sink. It was the colour of chicken soup and it smelt of hospital toilets but fucking hell, he thought, peering into the pan when the steam had cleared, it'd certainly done the trick.

*

Deb and that lot were watching telly too. Her hangover long

forgotten, Deb had been spurred into activity when she remembered the photocopies that she'd done at college the day before. She'd borrowed a book about Austin Osman Spare out of the college library and thought his weird automatic spirit drawings were fucking ace. She'd enlarged one of them up massive on the library photocopier, so it came out on about fifty sheets of paper like some gigantic fucking mosaic, and she and Tish had spent a couple of hours sticking them up on the wall; slowly piecing them together. It was like some sort of faceless monster rising up out of the pit and it looked great behind the sofa. When it were finished Tish went out to the shops, Sal had a bath, and Deb sat and smoked the last of the Black Sobranie.

'Fuck! Look at that!' said Sal when she came back in, pointing at the telly with one hand and smoothing down her freshly washed mohican with the other. She laughed as she did up the necklace made of strange runic beads with a bird's skull in the centre what she'd found up Ilkley when they'd been out mushrooming the previous year: 'Fuck the bloody Loyalist splin-ter groups! It's the fuckin Dogs of Thor innit, eh?'

'Oh aye, yeah!' cackled Deb. She was just about to launch into her imitation of Vlad Vargstrom when the door opened.

'What's this?' said Tish coming back in from the shops with some instant noodles for their tea.

Sal sighed her impatient, come-on-keep-up sigh:

'Northern fucking Ireland that's what...'

'No.' said Tish. 'Yeah I know that don't I. No. I mean what's this. I found it on the fucking step'

She put a cardboard box on the table. It were all taped up, and someone had written 'TO DEB FROM AN ADMIRER' on the top.

'Snot fuckin valentine's day zit?' said Deb. 'I wonder what it is then.'

Deb peered through the window to see if whoever'd left it was still out there. For a fleeting second she thought she saw the shadow of someone running down the alley out back, but it was too dark to tell.

'Well fuckin' open it then Deb!' Sal and Tish chorused in mock exasperation.

'Oh aye, yeah, alright then.'

She peeled away the tape and opened up the flaps on top of the box. For a second she recoiled in horror, but then she looked again at the strangely delicate, white object within.

'Fuckin ell, it's beautiful is that!' she exclaimed as she reached in to retrieve it.

'Aaaagh!' screamed Tish. 'Zit real d'you think?'

'Oh! Its lovely!' purred Deb. 'It must be from Pete. Them Sisters are right into this stuff! Eh, what d'you reckon, we can put it on the fuckin' mantlepiece, can't we, eh?'

'Sound,' said Tish and Sal in unison. 'Yeah that's sound is that.' Then they both watched nervously as Deb shifted some stuff to make a space for it and delicately placed the skull atop the fire place.

IV

Reginald C. Fellowes was a thoughtful and slightly troubled cleric in the noble tradition of thoughtful and slightly troubled clerics that had been sustained through the centuries by the good old C of E. His ruddy face and unkempt hair spoke of rather too great a love of the old blood-of-christ for a man in his position and perhaps, he reflected, as he locked up the Sacristy in the great old Cathedral that had been his home for some thirty years, that was what had got him into this mess. Quite why he should have deviated so wildly from his prepared speech at the annual Bishops' Dinner the previous evening he couldn't say, unless it could be put down to a decreased resistance to the wiles of old Bacchus that came with age and prodigious intake.

And now, knowing that a pack of burger-munching press photographers had taken up residence on the lawn outside his house in the Close, he'd taken refuge in the Cathedral building itself. They wouldn't dare to come in here, he knew that. And with his children long-since grown, and his wife living in sin with, for God's sake, some happy clappy Baptist minister in God-knows-where, there was no danger of anyone else being caused distress by the noisome and persistant paparazzi.

His parish priests had all been tremendously supportive, and that meant a great deal to Reginald C. Fellowes.

It was strange to think though of all the common criminals who'd sought refuge in the Cathedral during its thousand year history. The cut-purses and brigands who'd taken hold of the great brass knocker on the West Wing Door and claimed their God-given right to sanctuary; their fortnight of poncing off the Church, the ordering of their respective affairs, and the flight to France by sea had all been part of the package at one time. Jesus Christ! thought Fellowes to himself, how times have changed that he should now be the one seeking sanctuary.

Happened overseas of course, in Eastern Europe before the fall of the Berlin Wall, or in one of those damnable Latin American hell holes, but he couldn't remember an English Bishop ever having to seek sanctuary in his own Cathedral since Thomas a Beckett tried and failed at Canterbury.

He decided to seek the counsel of one who's advice he'd always sought through the greater part of his life. One who was always there and whose wisdom on matters both great and small could always be relied upon as from no other. But when he picked up the phone in the Vestry and rang the Cheshire nursing home where his mother was eking out her last days in a haze of dementia and popular songs of the pre-war period, the line was engaged. Damned luck!

He walked sadly down the Nave, admiring the stately grace of the ancient Norman columns, and muttering the words which had sealed Thomas a Beckett's death warrant: 'Who will rid me of this turbulent priest.'

'Oh God,' he cried out raising his arms high to the Cathedral's famous and justly celebrated stained glass windows, 'am I a turbulent priest too? A thorn in the flesh... sorry! A nuisance to be got rid of. A flea to be crushed on the back of this secular society, without even a second chance.'

He was taken aback when a harsh voice with a lilting accent that echoed around the elegant Gothic clerestory answered him back with a resounding 'Yes!'

Fellowes turned around, gazing up at the superb Baroque vaulting high above, which suddenly seemed to spin, as after some particularly heavy session on the old communion juice.

'Wh-who's there?' he asked timidly.

Suddenly the magnificent Tudor organ came to life, and as he looked around in bewilderment, Fellowes caught sight of some slight young figure with blonde hair perched high above the delicate carving of the Jacobean choir screen, who was really doing the most remarkable rendition of what had always been one of his favourite hymns. Rather too old-fashioned for the liking of most of his colleagues, it had none the less always spoken truly to Reginald C. Fellowes. But never more truly than it was about to.

'𝕭ringing in the sheaves, 𝕭ringing in the sheaves...' boomed the most exquisite baritone voice that Fellowes could ever recollect having heard. He span around again, and was relieved to see the figure of a cleric striding into the Nave from the Victorian-Gothic monstrosity which was known officially as the Railway Workers' Memorial Chapel, but which he'd always referred to rather scornfully as 'St Pancras Station'.

'𝕭ringing in the sheaves, 𝕭ringing in the sheaves...' And still the mysterious priest sang. He really did have the most remarkable and moving voice. And as he turned into the rock-hewn majesty of the Nave, Fellowes could see that the priest was carrying his crook before him. A bishop then. But not one whose voice he recognised. He would certainly know this voice again. It was miraculous, he reflected, a true gift, and it prompted him to say a quiet word of thanks to God for his marvellous works.

'𝕭ringing in the sheaves, 𝕭ringing in the sheaves...' As the unknown 'Bishop' neared, he stepped suddenly into the vast pool of golden light which was cast across the centre of the floor by the Roseate Window on the eastern end of the Transept. Fellowes had never been able to understand why this window had always proved to be the most popular postcard on sale in the Cathedral Gift Shop, though it certainly did cast an almost magical light on a glorious Autumn afternoon such as this one.

He looked again at the bearer of the voice, then audibly gasped. The man was dressed in pure white vestments from top to toe, but not only that, his skin and his hair were pure white as well. The only hint of colour were the eyes, the bright pink eyes which seemed to burn through Fellowes' skin, to see inside his very soul, and to condemn him without mercy for what was found there. For a moment he hoped that this was some sort of apparition. But as the White Welshman neared and resumed his singing, all the hairs on the back of Fellowes' neck stood up on end, and with another gasp he scrambled to his feet, running past the altar and down the East side of the Nave.

Beneath the early stone vaulting that had once under-pinned the original Norman clerestory he ran, finally taking refuge in the Lady Chapel near the great East Door. He'd always wondered why such a strange vestige of Popery remained in place in a protestant cathedral such as this, but now his doubts were forgotten and he frantically prayed to the Blessed Virgin Mary like a frightened choir boy who's being enjoyed up the arse by his Holy Father for the first time.

But it was no use, the booming voice which now seemed more a thing of terror than of beauty, was getting closer and closer, louder and louder.

'𝕭ringing in the sheaves, 𝕭ringing in the sheaves...'

And the footsteps of the voice's pallid owner were drawing closer too.

Fellowes, on his knees, looked over his shoulder and was terrified to see that this mysterious minister was not carrying an ordinary ceremonial Bishop's crook; he was carrying a scythe, which he swung rhythmically through the air like the muscular French farm labourers in some Courbet or other he'd once seen in Paris, couldn't for the life of him think which museum it was in though...

'𝕭ringing in the sheaves, 𝕭ringing in the sheaves...'

'Wh-what do you want?' he beseeched his pale persecutor. 'Wh-who are you?'

The white Welshman ignored his questions.

'Neither shalt though bring an abomination into thine house, lest thou be a cursed thing like it' Jeremiah Jones boomed. 'But thou shalt utterly detest it, and thou shalt utterly abhor it; for it is a cursed thing.'

'Oh for God's sake,' said Fellowes, in his best rank-pulling voice. 'As I explained to the Archbishop my remarks were taken entirely out of context... I merely indicated...'

'Before the cock crow thou shalt deny me thrice!'

Thundered Jones in reply.

Fellowes was dumbstruck. Who the hell was this weirdo. He certainly wasn't good old C of E that was for sure.

'Darest thou to be baptised as Jesus Christ was baptized in the holy waters of the River Jordan?'

Fellowes gaped in horror and was powerless to resist as the Welshman brought the scythe down on his neck. It was with some relief that he noted its broad edge was only resting lightly on his throat. But he wasn't prepared for what happened next.

'Oh God, no!' he screamed, as the pallid padre whipped out his staff of life.

'Annoint thyself with the blessed water of the Jordan River!' ordered Jones as he pointed his colourless cock at the felled man of God and directed the torrent of holy water into the terrified Bishop's mouth.

But Fellowes was having none of it. Fuelled by a sudden rush of righteous indignation he pushed up with all his might, surprising the Welshman, who fell backwards, winded, taking the handle of the scythe in the gut as he did so. Quickly Fellowes grabbed his chance, clambering up on to the statue of the Blessed Virgin and thence on to the high altar beyond. But the vengeful vicar was already back on his feet and swinging the scythe wildly at his legs, causing him to almost lose his balance. Fellowes looked around in desperation, suddenly seeing an escape route. Now! - he thought, as he launched himself at the rich, blue velvet curtain which was draped the entire height of the Lady Chapel wall - If I can only...

But Jeremiah Jones was too quick and lunged ahead of him with his lethal tool, blooding it on Fellowes' leg as it bit deep into the flesh.

'Thrust in thy sickle and reap!' he boomed triumphantly. 'For the time is come for thee to reap; for the harvest of the earth is ripe!'

Fellowes cried out in agony, then slipped and dropped awkwardly, somehow entangling himself in the luxurious golden rope with which the velvet curtain was embellished. His scream of terror was cut short in his throat as the coils of the exquisitely tasselled noose tightened around his neck. He fell quickly and was dead after one or two spastic jerks above the altar, a come stain spreading quickly across the front of his cassock.

Jones looked at his work, and he saw that it was good. But he gave a start, then turned and began to run as the blue velvet curtain was rent in twain by the considerable weight of the bouncing Bishop's body which fell down onto the altar with a sickening thump. And high above, a spear-shaped brass curtain rod rocked unsteadily then slipped off its mooring. As it fell earthwards, and just before it lanced through the body of the purple-faced Bishop, the great brass spear struck the enormous silver candlesticks which had graced the altar since the time of the civil war, and as they in turn toppled over, the dry and ancient velvet was quickly consumed by vengeful tongues of fire.

V

Bilko was kicking hizself. He wished that he'd stuck around the night before to see how Deb had expressed her love and gratitude to the man she surely knew was her only real admirer. The only one who really understood her.

He should have climbed up on top of the dustbins out back of her house and watched through the living room window as she opened his gift to her. Come to think of it though, he remembered now why he hadn't. The bins were overflowing with cartons of rotten milk and festering muck of all kinds. A rat had scurried out from behind one of the bin bags as he'd approached and he hadn't fancied seeing any more of them than was absolutely necessary. Not that rotten eggs and rodents were anything to get squeamish about. Not for him. They paled into insignificance by comparison with his escapades of two nights ago.

What the fuck had got into him? He shook his head and took an experimental drag on his tatty roll-up. Reaching for the lucifers he quickly got it going again. He just couldn't remember what was going through his head. What had possessed him to do it? To tell the truth it had all been a bit of a blur after he jacked up all the speed. His memory seemed to be composed entirely of unrelated fragments. Talking to Ron about Tibetan thigh bone trumpets. Watching Deb get chatted up by those losers. Getting thrown out by a couple of grebo bouncers. Walking through empty streets, silent except for the sound of distant laughter or the occasional drunken scream. He certainly couldn't remember having the bright idea to do that.

But once he had it must have been relatively easy to squeeze through a gap in the ancient iron railings that surround-ed the ruin of the old church near Woodhouse Moor. And once inside it had been a piece of piss to locate the old gardeners' store which was hidden behind a wooden door half-covered by corrugated iron at the foot of an ivy-clad buttress. He remembered pulling away the corrie and booting the door, how his foot had just gone straight through the rotten wood. There had been a selection of tools inside and all and he'd picked out a fairly solid-looking shovel.

Bilko glanced over at his bed. The handle of the shovel was sticking out from underneath it. He stomped over and booted it out of sight then sat back down and took an experimental drag on his roll-up.

'Bastard!' he shouted, throwing the cigarette across the room.

He'd gone tramping around through the ivy and brambles looking for a likely site. He had a flash of broken statues silhouetted against the moon. It was as if headless angels had been standing guard over his ungodly nocturnal deeds. If the church was now deconsecrated, did that apply to the angels too? Some of them were quite literally 'fallen' after all.

He remembered peering into the darkness behind some broken stones at the base of an ivy-clad obelisk, half expecting to find one staring back at him in the brief flaring light from the lucifer. But the inside of the obelisk had been empty and all he'd seen were bricks.

It wasn't as if he'd found it at all, come to think about it. Not really. It'd found him more like. He'd tripped over it cos it were hidden by the brambles and that. He'd broken the fall with the shovel and avoided whacking his head any road. Fuck, imagine that, he thought, knockin me-sen out and some copper finding me in the morning with a shovel in me hand. Jesus fuck!

Momentarily panic-stricken, he got up quickly and retrieved the rejected roll-up off the floor, re-lit it, then sat back down and puffed on it reflectively for a while.

He shook his head in disbelief at the thought of it all. You must be fucking mad, he thought to himself. Off your fucking tree. Probably still speeding out of your bonce from the gramme and a half, he reasoned, despite nodding out at the

Hell-Fire Club. Any road, that were probably just the impurities. And, since he was responsible for the fact that the speed had gained a good 50% more impurities since it'd come into his possession, he could personally vouch for its lack of quality.

Bilko remembered how, bracing himself against the shovel once he'd got his breath back, he'd found himself staring at a little headstone which surmounted a relatively bramble-free and grassy plot. He hadn't bothered to read the inscription; deciding quickly that he didn't want to know too much about the... well, he just didn't.

The shovel had bitten easily into the soft earth, and fuelled by impure speed and the fear of discovery he'd made rapid progress. He'd amused himself by having imaginary conversations with... thingy; 'I'm sorry. I don't think we've been introduced!'; or with some curious officer of the West Yorkshire Retropolitan Police Force, 'Evening, Constable. Is this the way to Australia?' They'd have locked him up and thrown away the key for sure.

He felt a rush of exhilaration at getting away with it, and took a celebratory swig from the can of ULTRA STRONG LAGER™ which was growing warm on the arm of his chair.

How long was he digging for? It was hard to say but it hadn't seemed to take very long at all before his shovel encountered something of a very different consistency to the soft earth above. He'd reached down and scraped away some soil with his fingers, then stamped experimentally on the wood. For the second time in one night his foot had just gone straight through. He'd pulled it out, suddenly feeling a wave of revulsion at the sweet'n'sour smell which wafted out from beneath the rotting, splintered wood. Then he'd just jimmied his shovel under it and torn it away, before reaching in to claim his prize. After that he couldn't remember a thing. How he'd got home without getting stopped was beyond him. With a municipal shovel over his shoulder and a grubby Morrisons' carrier in his paw... Jesus fuck! Maybe he just looked like a labourer on his way to an early start: 'Hi Ho, Hi Ho, it's off to...' Shit! It didn't bear thinking about.

He necked a final swig from the can and decided to go and pay Deb and that a visit. Play it cool like. He stubbed out the already dead roll-up and placed his hands resolutely on the chair arms. They were covered in a motley assortment of sticking plasters which did nothing to deaden the throb of the evil looking blisters beneath. Wincing with pain, he pushed himself up onto his feet.

*

'Deb it's for you!' shouted Tish into the house behind her. Fuck, thought Bilko to himself, she was huge. Her mass of back-combed hair made it necessary for her to bend her neck slightly as she stood there towering above him in the doorway. Her tits were massive and he couldn't take his eyes off her nipples which showed through the black silk of her top like a couple of thumbs.

He suddenly felt self-conscious and buried his plaster-encrusted hands deep in the pockets of his donkey jacket. He was buzzing with nervous excitement at the prospect of Deb finally recognising him for what he was and granting him the affection and gratitude which that recognition deserved.

Deb appeared in the hallway behind Tish, and as she peered around her shoulder Bilko could hardly contain himself.

'Hi ya Deb!' he chortled, then pulled himself together. 'Just come round on the off-chance like.'

Deb looked fantastic. Like death warmed up. Like a tragic yet beautiful character from some Edgar Allan Poe novel. Well, that were Jez's line; what Jez'd said when Bilko'd brought up the subject at the Hell-Fire the other night. And Edgar fuckin Allen whatever were the kind of stuff Jez'd be likely to read, so Bilko considered it'd do for him too. But as she peered past Tish into the night Bilko couldn't help but notice the vague flicker of disappointment that played across her perfect features. He pushed his glasses up the bridge of his nose and smiled.

'Oh, er, Bilko. How are yer.' said Deb.

'Yeah, sound, ta,' said Bilko. 'Just come round on the off-chance, like.'

'Yeah. You just said that!' said Deb, stifling a grin. 'Best come in then, eh.'

Bilko straightened up his shoulders. Deb'd smiled at him. Unmistakably smiled. He smiled back, but Deb had gone and he just got a glare back off Tish who then moved back off down the hall after Deb before turning and saying:

'We're through here.'

'What the fuck is that then?' asked Bilko, gobsmacked.

'Sa present from Pete, fuckin ace ain't it... Oh, that.'

Bilko was looking at the Austin Osman Spare drawing that covered the whole of the wall behind the sofa with his mouth open.

'It's Austin Osman Spare is that,' said Deb. 'Have you not heard of him?'

Bilko didn't want to show his ignorance.

'Er, yeah, yeah. I've heard of him like. S'just I never saw his stuff done this big like. What band's he in again.'

'No! He's dead. Fucking years ago. Zan artist wer'n'he. Spirit drawinz like. Spirits took over his hands and drew owt they wanted. He were just in a trance kind a thing.'

'Oh yeah,' shot back Bilko, trying not to blush. 'Oh yeah, I know who you're on about now. It's sound is that.'

'I got a book of 'em out the library at college,' said Deb, trying not to laugh as she picked it up off the table and pointed it at him. 'Here, have a look if you want.'

'Oh sound,' said Bilko, straightening his shoulders and taking up the offer. She'd smiled at him again. 'Ta.'

Tish was stood behind him, and she pulled a face as she pointed out the dandruff all over the shoulders of his donkey jacket. Deb stifled a laugh and covered it up by saying something. The first thing that came into her head:

'He's my favourite artist,' she blurted. 'Borrow it if you like.'

Bilko couldn't believe it, she'd smiled at him again.

He was looking at her with such a pathetic expression of gratitude on his bug-eyed face that she couldn't help really smiling this time:

'Yeah, go on. Borrow it. Only mek sure you give us it back, sovverdue intit.'

'Sound. Yeah, ta I will. Sound.'

Deb took the book off him and opened it up to a page that were marked.

'Look, some of 'em are brilliant. They'd mek great tattoos. Really different.'

'Eh!' said Sal who'd been ignoring Bilko in favour of the telly. 'Look.'

'And in a tragic accident today the Bishop of Derby was found dead in the smouldering ruins of Derby Cathedral. It's thought that he committed suicide following the outcry caused by remarks he made at the annual...'

'Thass yesterday's' said Bilko, nodding at the film of the burning cathedral that was running on the screen. 'Northern Ireland.'

'No. It's a different one. It's Derby. Fuckin ell!'

'Weird!' said Tish.

'Wicked!' said Deb.

'Sound!' said Bilko, pushing his glasses up his nose.

But Bilko's mind was on other things. He'd spotted the Festival of Night flyer on the table.

'What's this?'

'Oh, that. Yeah, sounds good doesn't it.'

'Whitby Abbey. What's that then?'

'Oh fuck Bilko. Have you not been there? It's fucking amazing. Thez this abbey on top of the cliff. Really spooky. S'where Dracula landed like, you know, in the book. Everyone's playing; The Sisters and that...'

'Sound,' said Bilko. 'Yeah, I wouldn't mind going to that me-sen.'

Then his attention wandered back to the matter in

hand. He closed the Austin Osman Spare book. So this was her favourite artist then was it. Somewhere in the back of his speed-raddled mind, a plan began to take shape. A plan that would have Deb flat on her back and begging him to give it to her. She'd smiled at him. Really smiled. She must be interested. He'd give her something to be interested in.

'Er, listen,' he said, shoving the book under his arm. 'I've gotta go like. Ta very much for the book though. It's sound. I'll bring it back round. Ta. Yeah.'

And with that he stumbled out of the room, narrowly avoiding walking into the door as he did so.

'Zmad in he!' cackled Tish as the front door slammed shut behind him.

'As a fuckin 'atter!' agreed Sal.

'Oh he's harmless enough!' said Deb. 'But yeah. Zoff is tree, in't he?'

VI

Vlad Vargstrom reached for his jacket. The chain-smoking English music journalist had been pumping him for ideas all afternoon, trying to get a bit of profile to back up a feature on the upcoming Festival of Night date that was the climax of The Dogs' forthcoming European tour. The smoke was bringing on one of Vargstrom's asthma attacks and, as he felt that familiar cramping beneath his ribs and began to fight for breath, he instinctively grabbed the handy medication supply from the pocket of the ancient looking leather that was draped over the back of a conveniently placed pine chair.

He took a puff and sat stock still for a second or two as the crashing pain in his lungs subsided, then suddenly relaxed and took a deep breath.

'Do you mind if the window I open?' he asked.

'Go ahead,' said the hack, making a mental note of Vargstrom's medical condition.

'Our Swedish air is good yah?'

The wordsmith ground out his duty free Marlborough Light then looked up at the satanic songster. Vlad Vargstrom looked like death warmed up. His T-shirt bore a reproduction of the famous suicide photograph of former Mayhem vocalist, Dead, lying on a bed with a shot gun in one hand and his brains in the other. Vargstrom's lank blonde hair framed a sallow complexion and only served to highlight the swastika-shaped scar on his forehead. Been reading too many Manson books, the hack thought to himself, suddenly despairing of getting enough material for the centre pages he'd been sent here to fill. The Dogs were big though, he knew that. Knew also that his readers would pay good money for a behind-the-scenes look at the men responsible for the top selling Sacreligious album. For himself though, he wasn't convinced that they weren't just jumping on the Norwegian Death Metal bandwagon. The tosser hadn't even heard of Whitby. In despair he'd given him the copy of Bram Stoker's Dracula that he'd brought along for background reading on the plane.

'So have you killed anyone lately?' asked the doubtful Londoner.

'There is a, how shall I say, like a war between the various bands in Norway, but here in Sweden we declare war just on Christianity. This is why our, um, musics are, um, about that.'

'Sacreligious, for example?'

'Yah, this is so. '𝕭𝖚𝖗𝖓 𝖙𝖍𝖊𝖎𝖗 𝖘𝖙𝖎𝖓𝖐𝖎𝖓𝖌 𝖈𝖍𝖚𝖗𝖈𝖍𝖊𝖘 𝖉𝖔𝖜𝖓!' Yah! Is good, no?'

The experienced hack was editing the interview down mentally before he committed the arcane squiggles of shorthand to paper, trying to make it a bit more angry. A bit more anything. Too fucking cheerful, he thought to himself. Too fucking cheerful by far. The readers back home wouldn't be fucking interested in this loser if they knew what the boring Swedish cunt was really like.

'Have you seen this...' he fished the previous two days' worth of English newspapers out of his flight bag, spreading them out on the pine table between them. Maybe he should try and get some controversial comments in. Make them up if necessary.

Vargstrom's face lit up.

'No. But I haven't now yah. These are English churches?' sing-songed the Swede.

'Well this one's in Northern Ireland,' said the hack, pointing at the dramatic photo of Belfast Roman Catholic Cathedral that graced the front page of The Times. 'But that one's in England, yeah.'

'Yah!' said the satanic Scandinavian enthusiastically. 'Is cool yah. Our English fans are werry, what you say, dedicated.'

'Yes they are!' the journo spat. 'Very dedicated.'

What a thick tosser, he thought to himself. Every inch the professional though, the hack was already setting out the page in his mind. For a start they could use a couple of big library pictures of the burning cathedrals. But what about the headline? 'The Dogs of Bore' was what he wanted to call it. And it was true enough and all, but the Editor would never go for it cos it would fuck the full page ad for Sacreligious in the next issue. Then he looked at the papers again and chuckled to himself, Vlad Vargstrom: 'Our Fans Did It!'

That was it. He jotted it down on the page, then had second thoughts and supressing a guffaw changed it to Vlad the Impaler: 'Our Fans Did It!'. Suddenly though, with the lightning reflexes of a seasoned press man, he put a line through the word 'Impaler' and replaced it.

Grinning to himself, he wound up the interview.

'Is good, yah?' said the grinning metal merchant.

'Very good,' nodded the self-satisfied reporter grabbing his flight bag. 'See you in Whitby!'

VII

North Yorkshire Echo
Monday September 14th 1999

'BAN FESTIVAL' PLEA
RESIDENTS IN 'PAGAN POP' OUTCRY

Worried Whitby residents yesterday handed in a petition calling for the cancellation of the so-called 'Festival of Night' rock festival which is scheduled to take place in the shadow of Whitby Abbey on the 31st of October: Halloween.

A spokesman for the protest group said: 'Whitby is a small fishing village with a reputation for being a place where people can come for peace and quiet. As well as being concerned about the large numbers of people expected, and questioning whether the council took questions of accomodation into account when they granted this 'pop festival' a licence, I just don't know how they can turn around and say that the amount of noise will 'not have a significant impact on the quality of life of local residents'. It's an outrage!'

A Council spokesman told us: 'Whitby is very dependent on tourism, and anything which brings in such large numbers of consumers can only be good for local business. In fact, it's worth pointing out that the numbers expected are roughly the same as would visit Whitby on an average August Bank Holiday' .

Local church leaders are also up-in-arms about some of the so-called 'Death Metal' bands taking part. The latest record from Swedish band 'The Dogs of Thor', who are headlining the festival, calls for the burning of churches. Clergymen fear that local youngsters might try and emulate this 'pagan' pop music.

Attempts by Echo reporters to contact the festival's organisers, Night Inc., at their London offices for comment were unsuccessful.

TURN TO PAGE 5

VIII

Vargstrom was looking at the map which had been pinned to the wall of their well-appointed Stockholm office by Olaf Jorgenson, the Dog's chain-smoking manager, in an attempt to foster the impression that he was some kind of international wheeler-dealer. Jorgenson was lighting a new cigarette from the butt of his last and blabbing away to the record company about publishing rights, and occasionally flicking to another call from Night Inc. that was holding on the second line. The fly on the wall, say, or the little mosquito that was buzzing around his head and at which occasionally he would take a swipe, would have seen that he was also studiously ignoring the presence of the celebrated satanic songster.

Jorgenson was a rock manager of the old school and was most famous in Sweden for being the man who'd turned down Abba. 'Boy-girl boy-girl will never sell. The fans will want you to be available! If I could split you up and have the girls sing Petula Clark songs... Now that I could sell!' had been his oft-reported comment as he'd shown them the door. He'd never made the same mistake again. In fact he'd never turned an act down since 1970, for fear of a fucking up in similar fashion. As a result he'd snapped up every no-hoper who'd ever been paraded before the once-attractive pine desk from behind which he conducted his business. At one point he'd had all the Swedish rights to a Norwegian tribute band to the ones who'd so famously got away: a boy-girl boy-girl outfit called The Norwegian Abba. But now, finally, it looked as if his desperate doctrine was paying off. The Dogs of Thor had originally come on to his books as a tribute band to Icelandic mould-breakers The Sugarcubes, who'd gone under the stage name of The Swedish Ice Cubes – but with a little careful grooming, a sacking here and a directional tweak there, he'd finally broken out of the holiday camp and jumble sale circuit which had been the band's bread and butter. And now it looked as if The Dogs of Thor were in prime position to step into the vacuum created by the imprisonment on murder charges of almost everybody connected with the Norwegian Death Metal scene. With the likes of Varg Vikernes banged up in jail, and a huge international audience in Europe and America baying for more satanic rock releases, Jorgenson was already planning how he'd spend the dosh that was surely about to come rolling in to the company. He'd signed the Dogs up for life in the kind of contract that went out of fashion with the abolition of slavery, and if those dumb fucks were content with pocket money, free booze and tattoos, his tastes were altogether more refined; his sauna needed repairing and his collection of early Twentieth Century furniture in the Swedish Style was far from complete.

Vlad Vargstrom was lost in thought as he absent-mindedly took a toot on his medication. He'd been reading, trying to read, the book which the English journalist had given him a few days before. And now he was looking at the big map of Europe trying to find Whitby. In the book, Dracula had chosen Whitby as the port of arrival on his journey to England. The crewless ship had sailed into harbour with the captain's corpse lashed to the wheel and a deadly cargo concealed in the hold: not just Count Dracula himself, but also thousands of black plague rats. This was good stuff. Vargstrom had become a Dracula fan overnight. There was definitely mileage in adding a bit of vampire mythology to the act. Bats and blood and shit. He turned to Jorgenson who was in the process of lighting a new cigarette from the butt of his last:

'Where is Vitby?'

'How the fuck should I know, you cock-sucker!' spat Jorgenson, holding his hand over the receiver to shield the music industry exec on the other end of the line from the obscenity. 'Look in the fucking atlas, yah?' Jorgenson pointed vaguely towards the bookshelf with his cigarette.

'Yah!' said Vargstrom, walking over to the the well-built

pine shelving and scanning the numerous volumes which confronted him there.

He pulled the atlas off the shelf and began to thumb through the index:

'Varrington, Vashington DC, Visconsin...' he whispered to himself as he worked his way down the list. 'Vitby! Yah, I have found it!'

Flicking back through the weighty reference book he quickly located the page which covered the largest part of England, turning back to the index to check the grid references for the object of his quest.

'D3,' he announced to no-one in particular as he returned to the map. 'D, D, D, D...' he muttered as he ran his fingers along the top of the page. '...3, 3, 3, 3,' he murmered as he scanned the right hand margin. Then, his search complete, he sat for a while in silent contemplation. There was not much to go on. A dot, with the word 'Whitby' beside it. His gaze wandered across the map. He found himself mouthing some of the place names silently, rolling them around on his tongue and enjoying the sound of the English:

'Heck-mond-vi-key', he intoned solemnly. 'Harley-fax, Hoodersveld.' Sure, they sang all of their material in English, but none of the band could really speak it. He wondered what it would be like to live in Essex.

Absent mindedly he thought again about the difficult interview with the English music hack, suddenly recalling the striking images of burning cathedrals from the newspapers.

'Belfast...' he mumbled, turning back to the index.

*

Bilko elbowed his way out of Pete Jaguar's shop and onto the street. It was late and the streets were dead except for the sounds of distant laughter and the occasional drunken scream. It was nearly done now and Pete had suggested they burn through the evening while it was quiet, and, cos it was all one colour, it had been progressing much more quickly than he thought it would. Despite his scruffy demeanour and the dirty oil-stained skin which made it look as if he'd spent his whole life stripping down motorbikes, Pete Jaguar was one of the best there was and if he couldn't do the drawings justice then Bilko didn't know who could.

Bilko'd had spent the best part of the last three days at Pete's and because of this he'd had plenty of time to read the story of Austin Osman Spare. He could see now why he was Deb's favourite artist. It was fucking ace work. And Bilko found himself particularly relating to the way that Spare had emptied his mind and just allowed the spirits to take over, to use the artist as an instrument of their will. It was like that was where ideas came from. If you were receptive enough. He wondered whether that was where his recent adventures had originated; in the realm of the spirits. Like the drugs had opened up his mind to other influences, new possibilities which had risen up in him from the beyond like the weird visions and creatures had for this Austin Osman Spare bloke. And, like an artist, he had acted upon them. No, he had allowed the spirits to act through him. He'd get a load more speed. Or perhaps it was the stuff he'd cut it with. He'd have to get the proportions right, to try and remember how much talcum powder and Ajax he'd mixed in.

It was the pain too. Something about it that seemed to switch his mind into another gear as he lay on the couch at Pete's place. It was like the buzzing just seemed to disappear and he went off into a weird sort of day dream. Just laying there and reading the book and that. Thinking. Thinking about all kind of weird stuff. It were like some kind of ritual, like in that film A Man Called Horse where the bloke gets hung up by his skin and that. And comes out somewhere beyond the pain as a true warrior or sommat. Yeah that was what it was like. Getting visions and stuff. Letting the spirits give you visions of the future and that. Visions of Deb sucking his cock in awestruck fashion when she'd seen what he done for her. Spreading her legs gratefully and saying 'Oh! Bilko! Fuck me now you bastard!' This was the future. The spirits had shown it him.

As he went down the steps to his basement flat and let himself in, Bilko was tempted to turn around and go over to Deb's place there and then. To show her, like. But then he thought better of it and decided to wait until it were finished. No point spoiling the surprise he thought. Best that she sees it all in full effect.

Slamming the door shut behind him, he gingerly took off his donkey jacket. This was no small feat, what with the state of his hands and everything else he was like a walking advertisement for the healing power not only of elastoplast, but also bog roll and sellotape. He went straight over to the fridge and took out a can of ULTRA STRONG LAGER™ cracked it open and necked some, drawing a sharp breath between his teeth before expressing his satisfaction. Easing himself gently down into the chair he fumbled for his Old Holborn, then pushed his glasses back up onto the bridge of his nose. Moments later he was striking up a lucifer and drawing the fragrant smoke deep into his lungs.

In full effect, he thought to himself smugly as he spat out a stray bit of tobacco. In full fucking effect.

*

Vlad Vargstrom had the office to himself at last. Olaf Jorgenson had gone for an extended meeting with the publicity people at the Dogs' record company. A slim excuse, generally, for a beer'n'coke binge that wouldn't be considered complete until they staggered out of Stockholm's only lap-dancing club at four or five in the morning.

Outside, the lights of the night time city burned brightly, but for once Vargstrom was not interested in the girls, the booze, the clubs. The fly on the wall, say, or that little mosquito that was buzzing around his head and at which occasionally he would take a swipe, would have been hard put to tell what he was up to, certainly he was lost in thought. He'd shifted a stylish pine occasional table from its usual position next to Jorgenson's dischevelled leather sofa, placing it beneath the map of Europe on the office wall. Grabbing a handful of drawing pins off the desk, he propped the atlas up on the table, then bent over to study first the open page of the atlas, then the corresponding area of the wall map. Pointing at Whitby with one hand he stretched up and found the corresponding point on the wall map, marking it with a drawing pin. He went through the same process for Belfast, then, for Derby. Ending up with three pins marking those places. Shrugging to himself he sat down and picked up the copy of Bram Stoker's Dracula.

*

Ron had been gone for about an hour. Since then Bilko had been sat at the table over a bathroom mirror with his head-shop dope scales in front of him and a razor blade in each hand, completely absorbed with the task in hand. He was cutting the speed Ron had delivered; mixing it with talcum powder and baking powder for bulk and Ajax for bite. He'd been a bit more careful than usual, trying to get it as close as possible to the last lot. Every now and then he'd stop and pare off a line with one of the blades then snort it, purely for quality control purposes. By the time he was satisfied with the result, he'd disposed of the best part of a gramme. Still, dealer's privilege, he thought. Plus there were still enough left to sell a few wraps, which'd more than pay for his. He tore a few pages out of an old TV guide and began to make the little origami packs. Folding the squares of paper in the time-honoured fashion and weighing out the grammes. He pushed his glasses back up his nose, choked down the bitter taste that was trickling down the back of his throat and then necked what was left of the ULTRA STRONG LAGER™.

It was only then that Bilko realised Ron'd left a copy of this week's NME as well as twenty grammes of ropey whizz. He picked it up and began to flick through it furiously. The speed he'd been snorting for the past half hour was really starting to kick in. His skin was tingling, and the crackling of plasters and sellotape beneath his clothes was starting to annoy him.

Hopping from foot to foot he found it hard to concentrate and after getting about half way through the music paper he gave up and put on his donkey jacket, then rolled the pop paper up very tightly and stuffed it in his pocket. Stopping only to gather up his Old Holborn and a couple more wraps of speed he was out the door and on his way to the pub within a matter of seconds.

*

The fax machine which sat atop Jorgenson's once attractive pine desk suddenly burst into activity. With a loud whirring noise it started to slowly spit out paper. The sudden blast of noise in the otherwise silent building was enough to snap Vargstrom out of his Bram Stoker inspired reverie. He been imagining himself, Vlad Vargstrom, sailing across the North Sea then gliding into a foggy Whitby harbour on a ship full of plague rats, having driven the crew stark staring mad or killed them. He put the book down then padded over to the desk in his shoeless feet and watched the sheets inching out of the machine.

It was nothing. Just a page or two of sketches from the designer. Sketches for some new banner for the tour. Simple. Bloody hammers crossed in the centre of a pentangle. Wolves in the centre of a pentangle. A swastika in the centre of a pentangle. Vargstrom glanced at them vacantly then dropped them in the tray and walked away from the desk. He'd almost picked up Dracula when he suddenly turned back and yanked the sheet out of the fax tray.

*

Bilko was nodded out where he sat in the Park Tavern. He'd talked about nothing but Austin fucking Osman Spare for a couple of hours, Ron hadn't been able to get a word in edgeways, just grunted every now and then while Bilko yammered on, chewing his mouth, pushing his glasses up his nose every two seconds and rolling cigarettes even when he had one in his mouth and another in the ashtray already. On and on he went. Spirits this and spirits that and letting visions rise up from fuck knows where and alluding to some big secret that was going to knock everyone out and blah blah blah blah blah. Pausing only to spit out the occasional stray bit of tobacco, he'd been like a man possessed, his eyes even more bugged out than usual. But then suddenly he'd just stopped in mid-sentence, and when Ron'd looked up to see if he were expected to grunt or just to nod he was surprised to see that Bilko was asleep, a fag in one hand and a pint in the other. Ron had thought about prising the tatty roll-up out from between his dirty fingers but figured that it had probably gone out of its own accord already - and wasn't there something about not waking up sleep-walkers or sommat? Not that Bilko was sleep-walking exactly, but Ron was glad of the break.

When they rang the bell for last orders, Ron made his way to join the money-waving throng at the bar, finally making it just before Time was called. As he turned, a couple of pints in his self-tattooed hands, he was surprised to see that Bilko was awake. Not only that, he was in the process of clambering onto the table. Hair and eyes more than just awry, Bilko was waving the centre pages of the NME around in one paw, and pointing at the reproduction Victorian map of the British Isles that was framed on the wall above him with the other. For a second Ron couldn't decide whether to go and get him down or to just pretend that he'd never seen Bilko before, and stand by while his mate got chucked out. Then, realising that the bar staff were still too busy to notice what was going on, he legged it over there, slopping beer down his jeans as he forced his way through the convivial crowd.

'Get off there Bilko you daft cunt. What you fucking doing?'

Bilko just gave him this wild-eyed look, then, as if he'd

suddenly woken up from a dream or sommat he looked down at the table which was wobbling beneath his feet and then up at Ron again before sheepishly climbing down and taking the pint which Ron thrust under his nose.

'What the fuck was all that about mate?'

Bilko just pointed at the crumpled centre pages.

'That!' he said. 'Just... just look at it will you.'

'Oh aye. It's bollocks is that. There's no way it were Dogs fans what did that.'

'No, no, I know it weren't. Look though. Them places. On the fucking map will you!'

Getting a distinct feeling that if he didn't look, Bilko would climb back up onto the table and show him, Ron dutifully got up and looked for Belfast and Derby on the map.

'Yeah. Belfast and Derby. What of it?'

'And Whitby!' screamed Bilko. 'And fucking Whitby and all.'

'Whitby? What's Whitby got to do with it?'

'It's not finished that's what. It's just not fucking finished.' spat Bilko, pushing his glasses back up onto the bridge of his nose. Then he sighed and let out a great fart before falling face first into the ashtray, knocking over his pint as he did so.

Ron rushed forward and prodded his arm:

'Bilko! Bilko!'

*

Vlad Vargstrom was sitting on the dirty shag piled floor of the office. The atlas was still open on his lap but his head was thrown back and he was snoring loudly. He was fast asleep.

Above him the map had been crudely ornamented. A single large pentangle had been scored repeatedly in crude and heavy lines across the British Isles. The fly on the wall, say, or that little mosquito that was buzzing around his head and at which he was well beyond taking a swipe, would have seen that the pentangle linked various towns. And if that mosquito had flown around the pentangle in an anti-clockwise direction starting from its south easterly apex instead of straight into Vargstrom's mouth, which instantly shut, it would have seen that those towns were Derby, Pwlheli, Belfast, Moffat and Whitby.

IX

'So, can you gerrus in or what then?'

Deb was getting straight to the point.

'Whassat?'

'Whitby! Can you gerrus in?'

'Probably. Don't see why not, yeah.' said Pete, vaguely and without looking up from his copy of that week's NME.

'Ace!' said Deb, grinning madly and starting to undo her top provocatively. She was looking forward to fucking him in his shabby little bedsit, wanted to add another date and venue to their tour. 'Come here then.'

'Hang on I'll just finish this,' Pete retorted, still glued to his music paper.

'What? You're going in a minute though!' she exclaimed.

Deb was dumbstruck, here she was offering the man who only a matter of days ago had described himself as 'An Admirer' the benefit of her considerable charms to liven up the moments before he went off to lug a load of flight cases and cables and gaffer tape and shit and he was more interested in reading the fucking NME.

'Yeah in a minute, I'll just finish this Dogs interview like.'

Rolling her eyes, Deb walked over to the table where Pete sat. She leant down and started kissing Pete's neck. He grunted quietly, evidently enjoying her affections but making no attempt to reciprocate them.

Deb raised her eyes to read the article, to see what was so fucking interesting that Pete preferred it to her. The Dogs interview was spread across the centre pages of the rag, framed by large colour photos of the flaming cathedrals. The headline across the top read:

VLAD THE INHALER: 'OUR FANS DID IT!'

Pete was mouthing the words silently to himself while he read. She kissed his unshaven cheek, then grabbed his long and dishevelled-looking pony tail and yanked it gently.

'Come on then!'

Realising that he wasn't going to get any peace until he'd satisfied the ungodly urges of the beautiful goth, Pete looked up at her. Before he could give voice to the 'Alright then' that was forming in his throat, she'd clamped her hot mouth on to his and stuck her tongue down his neck. They kissed long and deep, his hands moving enquiringly over her body, feeling her slender form shifting beneath the torn black silk of her top. She nibbled his ear and simultaneously grabbed his crotch with one hand. She could feel his cock expanding, getting hotter and hotter, harder and harder, extending itself and breaking out of her grip. Pete took a sharp intake of breath through his teeth before expressing his satisfaction. Then eager to exchange the sensation of silk for the warmth, softness and responsiveness of skin he slipped his hand down the front of her dress and began to caress her tits. When he lightly pinched one of her nipples it seemed to flick a switch in her cunt and she suddenly squirmed with the instant heat of her devilish desires. Deb sat herself down on the edge of the table then lifted one leg up and swung it over in front of him, placing her leather stilleto boot on the chair where he sat. Then she lifted up her skirt and grabbed his hand out of her top, placing it on the smooth skin of her thigh. Pete didn't need any further encouragement and his fingertips snaked up around her knickers, pulling them to one side in his eagerness to find the bitch's hot hell hole. He quickly pushed through the thick pubes that crowded around her cunt, then parted her quivering lips, pinching and stroking her clit with a demonic glint in his eye. For a moment she was still, a tiny moan issuing from her lips. But the way Pete was playing with her clit, sometimes softly, sometimes roughly, made her cunt so hot and wet that she could hardly think straight. Her lips were quivering for some cock action and when Pete slipped a finger up her arse, Deb reacted like a creature possessed. She sank her teeth into his neck and sucked till she could taste the bruise, while her other hand wrestled with his belt and flies to liberate his blood-filled love bone from the bounds of decency.

'Suck my cock!' he pleaded.

'Bugger that!' said Deb, allowing herself to fall back so she was lying on the table. She gathered up her skirts about her and then raised both legs, wrapping them around the roadie's shoulders. Then reaching down she grabbed his cock and guided it to the hairy gates of hades. The sight of her stockinged thighs and her hot and creamy cunt was all the encouragement the roadie needed.

'I wanna you to ride me to hell and back, you randy bastard!' she shouted as Pete impaled her with his enormous, veiny cock and, as if in reply, he drove it unerringly into the hot, pulsating heart of her being. Pete felt the walls of the under-world closing in on him as Deb writhed and howled beneath him like a banshee bitch on heat. As they both came the sights and sounds of Pete's shitty bedsit melted away, only to be replaced by a Bosch-like landscape of decadent and twisted desire; an empire of ungodly gratification populated by a host of demonic and unnatural creatures unbounded by the laws of nature. Deb and Pete had created a Garden of Earthly Delights and, as he shot what seemed like gallons of hot spunk into her convulsing cunt, they saw that it was good.

*

After two more evenings at Pete Panther's place, Bilko was all done. He'd walked home carefully, trying to avoid any sudden movements that might stretch his skin in surprising directions, trying to hold his body and arms stock still and let his legs do the work. He was completely oblivious to the waves of revulsion that his fleeting presence was invoking in any passer-by who happened to come too close. It'd been weeks since he'd washed, and now he was taking Pete's advice not to get them wet for a fortnight very seriously. If he got them wet, Pete had said, the scabs'd fall off and they'd take some of the ink with them. It was murder not to scratch them, but Pete had been similarly insistent on that point too.

He took a slight detour and pushed the Austin Osman Spare book through Deb-and-thats' letter box, then hurried stiffly off down the street before he bumped into any of them. That wouldn't do. It'd spoil the surprise. And he was saving that for the Hell Fire Club at the end of the week.

After letting himself in, he gingerly took off his donkey jacket, his jumper and his T-shirt. Unlaced the para boots, briefly turning his head at the wafts of decay that were suddenly released. He'd got the boots off the army surplus in the market and he hadn't noticed it at the time but they smelt like they'd been dug out of some mass grave in Srebra-fucking-nitza or somwhere. Then, after chucking the offending footware across the other side of the room, he undid his belt and slipped off his one pair of greasy jeans. Thus divested of his entire wardrobe, he padded restlessly around the flat in the alarmingly stained grundies beneath. They'd once have been describable as 'dirty' but they now read like a diary of Bilko's excretory habits; stain piled upon stain, like overlaid depictions of continental drift. Bilko collected skidmarks like other people collected stamps or records.

The entire upper half of his body was covered in bloody wads of bog paper, stuck on with sellotape. He looked like an advert for Andrex and it all rustled and creaked as he walked around. He stood in front of the mirror which were propped up on the junkshop sideboard, and tried to imagine what they would look like once the bog roll came off. It was hard to imagine. But one thing was for sure: when Deb saw it she'd be flat on her back!

It was a right pisser, his skin were so itchy that all he wanted to do were sit in a bath full of tepid water but he couldn't do that for fear of fucking-up Pete's work. In the end he decided to lay down on the bed. Within seconds he was fast asleep.

X

West Yorkshire Echo
Monday September 21st 1999

LEEDS GRAVE ROBBED
LATEST DESECRATION AT ST. CHADS

Council Workmen yesterday discovered a desecrated grave in the church yard of St. Chad's near Woodhouse Moor. A tool room had been broken into and it appeared that a shovel had also been stolen.

A spokesman for the West Yorkshire Retropolitan Police Force said: 'All we know is that at some point in the past week person or persons unknown have broken into the grave yard at St. Chad's and that a tomb has been opened. At present we are not disclosing the identity of the deceased until any surviving relatives can be traced. We would urge anyone with information to come forward, and can assure them that calls will be treated in strictest confidence and that they will not die mysteriously in custody.'

A Council spokesman told us: 'Obviously we do everything in our power to maintain local churches and to prevent acts of wanton vandalism such as this. Let's not forget that the dead paid Council Tax too, and we have a duty to ensure that an eternity spent in Leeds is every bit as enjoyable and rewarding as the usual 'three score years and ten'. We are currently liasing with the Police Committe to draw up a five point plan which we hope will prevent a repeat of this unfortunate and reprehensible incident' .

Leeds University Medical School emphatically denied that there is any shortage of bodies for Medical Students to study: 'This despicable act is not, repeat not, the work of some latter day Burke and Hare. But may we take this opportunity to remind Echo readers to carry their organ donor cards with them at all times.'

TURN TO PAGE 5

XI

With Pete and the other two roadies gone off to lug equipment in London for a couple of days, Deb and Tish and Sal were going off down the Hell Fire to get off their faces and raise some hell. It took them ages to get ready. Tish'd gone out to get some ULTRA STRONG LAGER™ for before they went, and they were supping away on their cans while they did their deathly white make up, back combed their hair and put on their black lipstick. Deb had treated herself to a new pack of Black Sobranie and, while Sal was regaling them with stories about how massive Andy's cock was and what a dirty fucker he was and all, Deb picked up the pack of lucifers that had been sat on the table for months. After rejecting one or two useless sticks of charcoal, she struck one and took a deep and slightly ostentatious drag then shook the acrid-smelling lucifer out and replaced it in the box. Then she sucked once more on the timelessly decadent cigarette, drawing the expensive tasting smoke deep into her lungs.

'He didn't!' Tish cackled.

'He fuckin did! I could hardly fuckin-well walk next day!' confirmed Sal.

'Come on, you ready then?' asked Deb.

'Aye,' agreed Sal. 'Come on Tish.'

*

As they walked into the club they looked like walking corpses with their white faces, black lips and them big black shadows round their eyes. With their tattoos and ripped up fishnets, their victorian whale bone corsets and their junkshop Whitby Jet jewellery they looked totally fucking wicked.

As they pushed their way out of the bogs and into the

crowded club someone shouted:

'Ey, it's the three fuckin' witches. Alright girls?'

'Yeah', cackled Sal, 'How's it going Ron.'

'Sound, ta,' said Ron, grinning. 'Eh, have you sin that Bilko yet?'

'No. Zee here then?'

'Aye,' confirmed Ron. 'And eez lookin for you and all. Said he had sommat to show you.'

'Snot what I've heard,' Tish cackled. 'I've heard eez not got much to show anyone.'

Sal and Deb joined in with the laughter. Ron looked slightly embarassed and said nothing. He had no worries in the trouser department, so the good looking goth girls' size-related banter didn't bother him as much as it would have if he was dimensionally challenged, but he wasn't about to get into a conversation about the size of his mate's love bone.

'Swot he said any road. That he had sommat to show you,' he retorted, testily.

'I'll look forward to that then!' sniggered Deb.

'Aye! We could do with a laff,' cackled Sal.

And with that they were off into the thick of it. The DJ was playing Siouxsie and the Banshees, and all thoughts of Bilko were dispelled. If he was looking for her that was bad enough, but she wasn't about to go and seek him out.

As it turned out she didn't need to. Pushing their way through the dance floor, the three tasty goth birds suddenly found themselves in some space.

'Christ all-fucking-mighty. What the fuck is that smell?' howled Tish in astonishment.

'Are the bogs leaking again?' asked Sal, suddenly remembering the day when the Hell Fire's overworked plumbing had given up the ghost and weeks-worth of shit and sanitary towels had rebelled against the forces of gravity. Clubbers had been slipping up on decaying tampons as they'd run for the doors.

'Oh! Jesus fuck!' exclaimed Deb, pointing in horror at

the figure who whirled dervish-like in the centre of the floor. 'Wossie gon an done now!'

Bilko was clad only in a pair of greasy jeans. As he whirled around on the dance floor he was oblivious to the waves of revulsion that were clearing the space around him, assuming that the jaw-dropping expressions on the faces of the clubbers was due to his new status as a face. He'd injected a couple of grammes of speed and was now doing the spirits' bidding. They were using him like a puppet and mekkin him dance like fuck. The epileptic way he jerked around it was as if he were getting shocks off some kind of high voltage stun gun, and a couple of bouncers were eyeing him in bemusement, unsure whether to boot him out or summon medical help. One or two Japanese goths – all thoughts of cool detachment gone – were staring at him in pure, open-mouthed amazement.

Suddenly Bilko stopped dancing and swayed unsteadily on the dance floor, like it were the deck of a ship and he hadn't got his sea legs yet. Pushing his glasses up his nose he suddenly caught sight of a familiar and stunningly beautiful face looming out at him from the crowds. It was Deb. He waved cockily and walked over.

As he did so, Deb suddenly found herself trying to step back, but the crowd of people gawping at Bilko's tats prevented her from moving. The DJ was playing a rave-from-the-grave; *Come to Daddy* by the Virgin Prunes, and the combination of that and Bilko's leeringly goggle-eyed stare was truly terrifying.

'Bilko!' she stammered. 'What the fuck have you done?'

Bilko took an experimental puff on his tatty roll up. It had gone out.

Come to Daddy.

'Have you got a light Deb,' he asked, revelling in what he supposed was her lustful approval.

Deb rummaged in her bag and pulled out a box of lucifers, then discarded a few useless sticks of charcoal before striking one and offering Bilko the flame. As he drew the smoke into his lungs and spat out a stray piece of tobacco, Deb shook out the acrid-smelling lucifer and replaced it in the box.

'Bilko!'

'Sostin fuckin Spare intit!' he said proudly.

Come to Daddy.

Deb forced herself to look at Bilko's pasty body. Every inch of his arms and torso were covered in black drawings. Weird spirit entities and demons seemed to be rising up from the pit. She felt like she was tripping. The drawings looked almost alive. As if any second they would begin to moan and wail out their centuries of anguish. He'd had the entire works of Austin Osman Spare drawn onto his body, and the result was more peculiar than revolting, though revolting it certainly was. She didn't know which face to look at.

'Pete Panther did it!' Bilko added. Certain now that Deb would succumb to her long-supressed desire for his cock.

'They're real?' Deb screamed in confusion. 'You mean, they're fuckin tats?'

'Yeah, sound intit!' Bilko beamed. He was speeding off his face and now that he'd stopped dancing he had no choice but to yammer. 'You said they'd make great tats, and I thought, well you know, the spirits made me think, d'you know what I mean, I know where ideas come from Deb, so they acted through me or whatever, well, I thought, you know, yeah, you're right, I suppose they would, and the spirits showed me the way like, and I did it for you Deb, but he's my favourite artist too, now, and I couldn't decide which one to have done like and in the end I thought, well fuck it, do the fuckin lot, an Pete Panther were right into it and all, iss tekken a couple a weeks to do, like, but...'

As Bilko looked down at the plethora of inky faces which covered his body, momentarily hypnotised by the unearthly fizzogs which seemed to move and blur before his eyes, Deb took her chance and backed away. Slowly at first, one step at a time, then she just turned and ran into the crowd, and did-n't stop till she found herself, panting, at the bus stop down the road.

Come to Daddy.

The Virgin Prunes song was echoing in her head, and hideous demonic faces danced before her eyes, but none was more hideous than Bilko's knowing leer. He did it for her! What the fuck was he talking about? He thought she'd be impressed or sommat. UGH!.

Come to Daddy.

He's fuckin lost it, she thought. Completely fuckin lost it.

XII

'Amen' chorused the acolytes as one.

'And in the midst of the seven candlesticks was one like unto the Son of man, clothed with a garment down to the foot, and girt about the paps with a golden girdle. His head and his hairs were white like wool, as white as snow; and his eyes were as a flame of fire...'

Jeremiah Jones was holding forth to the bowed heads of his flock.

'Amen,' they chorused once more, and as one they trembled to recognise the pigmentless preacher in the words of the holy scripture.

'One among us has sinned!' boomed Jones. Momentarily lifting his eyes from the open bible in front of him and scanning the ranks of attractive disciples laid out before him until his eyes lit upon the one who seemed more shamed than the rest.

'Brother Jonathan!' he roared. 'Brother Jonathan! Do you dare to come before christ and murder love?'

The object of his gaze visibly shuddered, then, wracked with guilt and weak beneath the forces of righteousness his body suddenly convulsed and he vomitted bile onto the floor in front of him.

'For that is what you have done, Brother Jonathan! You have murdered Christ's love. Verily I say that you may as well have driven the nails into His hands yourself!'

'Amen,' came the rejoinder from the supplicant disciples.

Brother Jonathan wiped his mouth with his sleeve and sobbed.

The melanin-deficient minister reached down and picked something up from his pulpit. It was a copy of last week's NME.

With fire in his eyes, Jones waved the music paper in the air above him, then, reducing his voice to a mere whisper he enunciated the sins of Brother Jonathan.

'Dearly beloved,' he murmured. 'My children. How canst though forsake me so? Lord, forgive Brother Jonathan, he knows not what he does. Satan hath tempted him with thoughts of earthly pleasures, and with the songs of...'

He brandished the NME in the air above his head and turned up the volume.

'...the devil himself! He hath brought these abominations into the house of the Lord, and he shall burn!'

Brother Jonathan looked up in horror. He'd brought a copy of the NME in town and hidden it in his bedroom. Jones had discovered it and now he would certainly go to hell. He had sinned. He had been tempted by the Mother of Harlots and forsaken Christ's love and deserved to burn in hell for the rest of eternity. He convulsed once more and bitter liquid spewed forth from his unclean body.

'But,' Jones was speaking in a whisper again, and the apostles of the albino strained forward to hear the words of truth he would utter. 'But the Lord our God works in mysterious ways. For it was He who directed Brother Jonathan to this vile epistle from hell itself. It was He who made Brother Jonathan hide this abomination where He knew that his humble servant would find it. For the Lord thy God hath shown me the way. The Lord thy God hath shown me the truth and the light. And the Lord they God hath shown me THIS!'

Jones pointed at a full page ad in the back of the high-selling pop weekly.

'The Lord thy God hath acted through our beloved Brother Jonathan and he hath shown me that the Devil's work is never done. WHAT ABOMINATION IS THIS?' he thundered, repeatedly jabbing the page with his deathly digit. 'I'll tell you: it is a festival of NIGHT! a festival of SIN! a festival of EVIL! and a festival of THE DEVIL! Thank you, Lord, for blessing

Brother Jonathan and allowing him to show us thy purpose.'

Brother Jonathan was reeling. He'd been pulled back from the brink of eternal damnation. His mortal mind was unable to compute this sudden change in his spiritual fortunes and, letting out a great fart, he fainted.

'Brothers and Sisters,' boomed the Welshman. 'Bring him forth that he might be blessed with the Love of God and the fellowship of the holy spirit!'

Had Brother Jonathan been conscious he would have felt the hands of many being laid upon him. Felt himself lifted up and carried onto the altar. Felt his wrists and ankles being tied to the four corners thereof. Felt the hands divest him of his earthly clothing and render him naked in the eyes of the Lord.

'Gather round ye faithful,' intoned Jones, 'and let us baptise our Brother in the name of God'

As one, the acolytes parted their robes.

Brother Jonathan awoke to find a Sister squatting above his face, she reached down with one hand and parted the golden curls that surrounded her heavenly hole. He watched as she slyly fingered her clit, rubbing it into a quick and red arousal. He strained against his bonds and tried to lick her cunt. He could smell the love juice that was beginning to boil up from her hot hole and he saw that it was good. Then she let loose with the waters of the holy river Jordan. Averting his face from the hot, sweet gush of piss he saw that he was surrounded with Love, and he felt the warm waters of Jordan splashing onto his skin from every side as each of them anointed him.

As the last drops were squeezed and shaken out, and the piss began to pool beneath him, he suddenly felt cold, and shivered uncontrollably.

'Turn our beloved brother around, that he might be fully blessed,' Jones commanded. The disciples crowded around and loosed the straps with which Jonathan was bound, before roughly rolling him onto his stomach and re-tightening them.

With a wave of his hand Jeremiah Jones signalled the organist to begin playing. It wasn't Christmas, but the hymn for today was O Come All ye Faithful, and as the strains of the introduction faded away, Jones bade his acolytes to join him in song.

'Now Brother Jonathan, are you ready to receive the body of Christ that you may enter the kingdom of Heaven?'

Jonathan nodded his head. He wanted to be saved. He didn't want to burn in hell for all eternity. He felt a light rush of wind on the backs of his legs as Jones's divested himself of his white robes, and loosened his golden belt, felt it stinging his buttocks once, then twice. Then, as the singing supplicants reached the crescendo of the much-loved Christmas carol's chorus Jones thrust the staff of life deep into his disciple's arse and began to pump away in time to the uplifting organ music.

'Ah! Ah! Ah!' groaned the pallid preacher.

'Oof! Oof! Oof!' grunted Brother Jonathan.

'Aaaaagh!' screamed Jeremiah Jones as he pumped the obedient arse of his disciple and the Love of God boiled in his balls.

'Receive ye...' he bellowed at the body of the supplicant who was stretched out before him. 'Receive ye the Holy Ghost! Whosoever sins ye remit, they are remitted unto them; and whosoever sins ye retain, they are retained. Verily, verily I say unto thee, when thou wast young, thou girdest thyself, and walkedst whither thou wouldest: but when thou shalt be old, thou – shalt – stretch – forth – thy ...UMFFFFF!' and with that, what seemed like gallons of hot and creamy christian cum shot deep into the acolyte's arsehole.

*

Later that afternoon Jones was seated at his desk, the telephone receiver in his hand. The oak-panelled office smelt heavily of the frankincense which was burning in an ornate golden censer on the windowsill. The rich autumn sunlight was streaming in through the window and, momentarily distracted from the distant-sounding and heavily accented voice which was talking at the other end of the line. Jones paused to wonder at the marvel of His works. '𝕬𝖑𝖑 𝖙𝖍𝖎𝖓𝖌𝖘 𝖇𝖗𝖎𝖌𝖍𝖙 𝖆𝖓𝖉 𝖇𝖊𝖆𝖚𝖙𝖎𝖋𝖚𝖑,' he thought to himself, '𝕬𝖑𝖑 𝖈𝖗𝖊𝖆𝖙𝖚𝖗𝖊𝖘 𝖌𝖗𝖊𝖆𝖙 𝖆𝖓𝖉 𝖘𝖒𝖆𝖑𝖑.' Then he returned to the matter in hand, and jotted some notes in a file that was open on the desk before him, then hung up the phone. He picked up the file and wandered through to his 'inner sanctum'; the library. Looking like little more than a large cupboard, the library was in fact a humidity controlled strong-room, built to withstand a nuclear blast, and it housed one of the largest collections of Satanic material ever assembled in the world. A fax machine sat on a small desk against the back wall, and a whole sheaf of paper had collected in the output tray. Jones scanned through the faxes, which had come from as far afield as South America and the Arctic Circle. He then bundled them under one arm and surveyed his works. One entire shelf of the library was devoted to the collected correspondence of Alister Crowley, Jones had paid an arm and a leg for various job-lots of contraband Crowley, but it'd been worth every penny. He also had original copies of Anton LaVey's hand-written manuscripts, a number of Austin Osman Spare drawings, the entire output of Thee Temple of Psychic Youth (ranging from xeroxed anti-propaganda bulletins, to home-made cassettes of Genesis P.Orridge singing along to Velvet Underground records when he was training his voice for the Force The Hand of Chance album, to a number of carefully reconstructed and total-ly demonic 'dream machines'), to copies of every goth, death, and heavy metal album ever made. To the observer, Jones's amassing of the most inclusive archive of Satanic art and literature in Europe might have seemed perverse, un-Christian even. But that wasn't how Jeremiah Jones saw things: 'know thine enemy' was one of his mottos in life.

'𝕺𝖓𝖜𝖆𝖗𝖉 𝕮𝖍𝖗𝖎𝖘𝖙𝖎𝖆𝖓 𝕾𝖔𝖑𝖉𝖎𝖊𝖗𝖘,' he hummed, dropping the file into the open drawer of a filing cabinet before closing and locking it, '𝕸𝖆𝖗𝖈𝖍𝖎𝖓𝖌 𝖆𝖘 𝖙𝖔 𝖂𝖆𝖗.' His business done, he returned to the relatively wide-open space of his office, first attending to the task of locking the solid metal library door. It wouldn't do for any of his innocent acolytes to wander in here, this was the kind of material that could drive people to the very brink of insanity. Plus he didn't want anyone to know about the other little line of business which was conducted within the two foot thick concrete walls of his library.

Sitting back down at his desk he whipped a calculator out of the desk drawer and did a few sums, making a note of them in a large notebook before triumphantly muttering, 'Yes!' to himself and underscoring the figures that were the result of his righteous arithmetic.

He ripped the sheet from his note pad and walked briskly across the room to the door. Opening it, he looked once more at the notes he'd scribbled before dashing quickly down the corridor.

As he strode into the church, the eyes of his flock turned to watch the imposing figure of the White Welshman take his place at the pulpit once more. It'd been a long day. They'd all been at prayer since seven in the morning, and for the past five hours they'd been standing in silence. One or two had fainted where they stood and now were asleep on the floor. But the presence of the pale preacher was enough to see them struggling to their feet. 'Forty days and forty nights our saviour didst fast in the wilderness,' he'd say on occasions such as these, 'And ye cannot even manage forty minutes. Oh ye of little faith!'.

He signalled one of his acolytes to switch on the overhead projector. An acetate xerox of the top-selling music paper's ad for the Festival of Night was thrown against the screen to the right of the altar.

'Get thee behind me Satan!' screamed Jeremiah Jones.

'Amen,' came the tired chorus in return.

Signalling the acolyte to change the transparency for one which focused in on the name of the festival's headline act, Jones then expounded his afternoon's work. Numerologically speaking, he explained, the value of the name of that unholy alliance which is called 'The Dogs of Thor' was 3,996. Subtract from this the year in which the band released their first single and divide the result by the Holy Trinity – the Father, the Son and the Holy Ghost – and, lo, you get 666.66666 recurring.

'Let him that hath wisdom,' he intoned, 'reckon the number of the beast: for it is the number of a man; and his number is six hundred and sixty six.'

He pointed at the words on the screen.

'These so-called Dogs of Thor are not the devil, but verily I say unto you that these are an abomination in the eyes of the Lord, for they do the work of the beast and they are as unto the number of the beast. 'Who is like unto the Beast?' the Lord asks. And I say to you that these devil-worshippers carry his number within their withered hearts. Therefore I say we must smite them down. Yeah, children, the last days are verily upon us. The works of the Beast are all around us. He who hath ears let him hear, for the day of judgement is at hand. And the seven angels which have the seven trumpets shall prepare themselves to sound. The first angel shall sound and there shall follow hail and fire mingled with blood, and they shall be cast upon the earth, and the third part of the trees shall be burnt up and all green grass shall be burnt up. And the second angel shall sound and a great mountain burning with fire shall be cast into the sea, and the third part of the sea shall be turned to blood. And the third angel shall sound and there shall fall a great star from the Heavens and the name of the star shall be Wormwood and the third part of the waters shall be made bitter and many men shall die from drinking thereof. And the fourth angel shall sound and the third part of the sun shall be smitten, and the third part of the moon shall be smitten and the third part of the stars and the day shall not shine for the third part of it and the night likewise. And an angel shall fly through the midst of heaven and cry Woe, woe woe to the inhabiters of the earth by reason of the other voices of the trumpet of the three angels which are yet to sound!'

'Amen,' murmured the exhausted apostles of the albino leader of the Church of the Everlasting Day.

XII

Bilko staggered out of the club. He was still speeding out of his fucking box when kicking-out time came around. He'd spent the best part of the last couple of hours racing round the Hell Fire looking for Deb. Sal and Tish were still there, he could hear them cackling practically everywhere he'd gone, but there were no sign of Deb. He pulled his T-shirt over his head and stuffed his arms in the sleeves of his donkey jacket. He couldn't work out what had come over Deb. Perhaps she'd been tripping and had got paranoid or sommat. Maybe she was afraid to act upon the desires which must surely be consuming her. Some people were afraid of real feelings, preferred the safety of casual fucks to the deep and stormy seas of passion. Maybe he'd misjudged her, but he thought not. He could understand her; knew that her relationship with the realm of the spirits was as real as his.

    Bilko trudged homewards. The streets were dead except for some distant laughter and the occasional drunken scream. Pulling his donkey jacket tight against the cool autumn night, he pushed to the back of his mind the niggling thought that perhaps she didn't fancy him. Of course she did. He could see it in her eyes as she'd gazed at the tattoos he'd had done for her. Knew that she'd been dying to jump on his hot hard cock. Perhaps it had been the wrong place to show her. Perhaps that was why she'd run off. Cos she was afraid to show her true feelings in front of such a large audience. Perhaps she'd run to the bogs and had a frantic wank just to try and keep her feelings under control. The thought of Deb with her skirt lifted up and one foot on the bog, squeezing her tits with one hand while the other caressed her hot and knickerless cunt was almost too much for him. He imagined Deb frigging herself off, whispering his name through clenched teeth as she came. That must have been it. It was a vision from the spirit realm. That's what she'd done. She must have. No wonder she'd legged it so quickly. Waves of love and desire washed over him as he trotted down the steps and let himself into the basement flat.

Once inside he chucked his donkey jacket on the bed, then went over to the fridge and pulled out one of the cans of ULTRA STRONG LAGER ™ that he'd stocked up on so he'd have been able to offer Deb something to drink when she came home with him. Reaching under the carpet next to the firepace he pulled out a wrap of speed. Once he was comfortably esconced in his chair, Bilko cracked open the can, then, balancing it on the chair arm, he carefully unfolded the wrap and tipped the contents, a half-gramme of whizz, into the lager. Then, as an afterthought, he scrunched up the empty origami square and popped that in too, so as not to waste any. Once this was done he pulled out his Old Holborn and a packet of red Rizla papers. Moments later he was striking an acrid-smelling lucifer and lighting a tatty roll-up, pausing only to spit out a stray bit of tobacco. Picking up the can of ULTRA STRONG LAGER™ he drained half of it, then took a sharp intake of breath through his teeth before loudly expressing his satisfaction. It didn't take the speed long to soak through the lining of his gut and top up the stuff he'd done earlier.

*

Vlad Vargstrom was like a man possessed. He'd been working all night to plan the Dogs of Thor's spectacular entrance on the last night of the festival in Whitby. Olaf Jorgenson had been on the case that day too, and firmed up the arrangements with Night Inc., the festival promoters. And now it was done. Vargstrom had been doodling on a pad, just working on the detail. Planning how to make the biggest impact. It was all thanks to the English journalist. He'd planted the seed of the idea when he'd given Vlad his copy of Bram Stoker's Dracula. But it was Vargstrom's Nordic determination that had carried the idea to near-fruition. Jorgenson had loved it, of course.

Anything that would help to sell records was alright by him.

Vargstrom yawned, and decided that enough was enough. He'd go and get some sleep now. But on the way out of the office, while he was switching off the lights, he glanced up at the map he'd worked on the previous week. Jorgenson hadn't bothered to take it down, or to change it. He'd said he quite liked the heavily drawn pentangle that was scrawled across the British Isles.

Vargstrom walked over and pulled the map off the wall. Then he placed it down on Jorgenson's desk and ran his fingers along his own embellishments, tracing out the five pointed symbol which had so many meanings. Something caught his eye on the floor. He reached down and grabbed the box of lucifers which must've dropped out of the Dogs' chain-smoking manager's pocket earlier on in the day. Striking one of them he held the flaming end against the city of Belfast, then moved it around to ignite the paper where the word Derby was still visible beneath his heavy black lines. As the flames licked up the tiny lucifer he quickly shook it out and struck another. This he held against the northernmost point of the pentagram – some place called Moffat – before quickly lighting the paper beneath a tiny peninsula in North Wales, then, trying not to burn himself, he applied the flame to Whitby.

Vargstrom watched mesmerised. For a split second – before the fire took hold of the paper, before it crinkled up and turned into ash – the whole of the British Isles was mapped out beneath a flaming pentagram. The fire spread quickly though, radiating out from the British Isles in an ever larger circle of destruction. Panicking suddenly that the sprinkler system might auto-activate, Vargstrom up-ended the vase of flowers which sat at one end of the desk, extinguishing the flames in an instant.

*

He couldn't tell how long he'd been asleep. Maybe it was minutes or maybe it was hours. It were still dark outside, and

Bilko could feel the spirits calling him. He was suddenly alert; the whizz still doing its relentless stuff. Something had happened while he slept. Like Austin Osman Spare, he'd opened his mind to the other side and now he could feel new ideas forming in his brain, could almost hear the electrical activity that was going on in there. For a sudden heart-stopping moment he realised the truth about Deb. He hadn't done enough to win her over. Something would have to be done. Something drastic. He allowed the spirits to conjure up pictures in his brain. Willed them to act through him. Like a sort of artist he'd allow their ideas to inhabit him, then sort of act them out. In a blinding flash he knew what he had to do. Only two things. Two beautifully evil things. He'd make Deb want him so much that her cunt would be hot and quivering for his cock 24 hours a day. She'd not be able to rest until she impaled herself on his throbbing love bone. He'd make sure of that. Right now though, in order to put his plan into effect, there were a couple of things he'd need. He grabbed his donkey jacket off the bed and legged it out the door without even stopping to pick up his packet of Old Holborn.

XIV

Come to Daaaaaaaddy.

Deb woke up with a start. Her heart were pounding and she sat quickly up in bed, then, realising that it had just been a dream she laid back and stared at the ceiling. She'd been at a Virgin Prunes gig, in her dream, only Bilko'd been the front man and he'd been pointing at her while he sang and behind him the rest of the bands' faces had been melting away only to be replaced by anguished visions of creatures from another realm. But it were just a dream. Thank fuck for that, she thought as she heard movement downstairs.

'Oh fuck!'

That were Sal. She was usually first up.

Deb threw back the covers and eased herself out of the bed, her pale skin illuminated by the daylight from the window. It was cold and her skin was instantly covered in a dusting of goose bumps, her nipples hard. Her top floor bedroom looked out onto a windowless gable end opposite so she seldom drew the curtains.

Walking naked over to the window Deb stared out at the city which was going about its business pretty much as usual. She wondered what time it was. Late, presumably. Running one hand down across her breast, Deb pinched her nipple delicately between thumb and forefinger. Pete and that were due back today. Good. The thought of Pete's cock pumping her hot arse made her cunt twinge in anticipation. She pinched her nipple again, then flicked it; flicked the other one. It seemed to turn a switch in her cunt, which was instantly creamy. She ran her fingers down until they encountered her thick black bush, then quickly parted her lips, exposing her clit to the cold touch of air and finger. Still lightly flicking her tits with one hand, she pinched and pulled at her clit a few times before settling into a good, steady rhythm.

Deb's cunt was so hungry for action that she knew she'd not be able to sit still till she'd had a bone-shaking cum – with or without the aid of Pete's cock. She turned on the electric fire and got back into bed, enjoying the burning fluff smell as the elements quickly heated up. It were still warm under the covers. Spreading her legs wide apart, it didn't take very long to pick up where she'd left off; slowly circling two fingers around her stiff clit, sometimes gently, sometimes more roughly. She closed her eyes and imagined Pete's blood-filled love bone bouncing around in front of her face; grabbing it with one hand then stretching out her tongue to lick the purple tip, which would be as hard and shiney as a pebble worn smooth by countless centuries in the ocean. Then she'd relax her jaw and take in the full length of his veiny cock, gagging on it as she bobbed her head up and down, lightly grazing its base with her teeth.

Her fingers started to move faster, more insistently, and her hot cunt's gush-rate increased to match.

He'd turn her round then, and climb on top of her. No. That wasn't gonna do it. Deb turned herself over, so instead of lying on her back she was crouching on all fours like some kind of hot and horny bitch. Spreading her legs so that her cunt and arse were exposed, she arranged herself so that her face was lying sideways-on against the pillow, her tits pressed against the sheet. She loved being fucked like this. With her arse up in the air. With one hand she resumed her fingerwork, while in her mind's eye Pete – who was occasionally interchangeable with a big black dog – was pumping his thick and veiny cock into her cunt. 'I wanna be ridden to hell and back you horny bastard!' she thought as she pushed back again and again and imagined his hot length being driven unerringly into the hot, pulsating heart of her being while she writhed and howled like a banshee bitch on heat. As her pelvis and thighs started to shudder she redoubled her efforts, pinching her nipples hard with her free hand. Suddenly the sights and sounds of her fantasy melted away only to be replaced by a Bosch-like landscape of decadent and twisted desire; an empire of ungodly gratification. Deb had created a Garden of Earthly Delights and, as she threw her head from side to side and came loudly through gritted teeth, she saw that it was good.

*

Bilko wandered down the aisle of the National Express coach, finally selecting a seat at the back, next to the bog. A hand-written sign had been taped on the toilet door, which simply said 'Out of Order'. He stowed his bag under the seat then settled back to enjoy the journey. It'd been a while since he'd had a holiday, Bilko reflected, as he looked out the window at the bus station beyond.

He'd raided his emergency stash. Been to the building society first thing and taken out the lot. All them rent cheques that were still sent to his mate's former house regular as clockwork and which, with a nicked lecky bill, he'd been able to use to open an account. He'd borrowed the keys once when his mate were away and needed someone to feed the cat. Bilko, thinking ahead for once, had got a spare set made and nicked Danny's NHS Card. They were still accepted as proof of identity, but it'd not be the kind of thing Danny'd notice was missing. Then when his mate'd fucked off to Amsterdam a few months later Bilko'd let himself in to see what he could see. He were glad of it now. He'd not touched it before. All the cash he had at the house were what he owed Ron from selling the speed, and he couldn't touch that.

If anyone had seen him coming out of the bus station bogs, anyone who knew him that is, they'd probably not have recognised him; Bilko was a man transformed. It were the spirits that did it. It were their idea. That he shouldn't be too noticeable. He'd set aside some of Danny's cash for clothes; bought a new pair of black Levi's, a couple of new black T-shirts, traded in his donkey jacket for an army surplus parka, and invested in a new pair of cherry red Docs. Arriving at the bus station he'd headed straight for the 'executive restroom' (ha ha) with its shower facilities. He bought a vending machine shaving kit, and a disposable toothbrush. Then stood under the shower's warm jets, felt the water pummelling his skin. Twenty minutes later he'd reappeared; slicked back hair, clean shaven, clean clothes - a new man. Even his old, thick-framed glasses looked trendy. Trendy-ish. He'd stuffed the old Bilko into a bin and run for the coach.

He reached down and pulled a can of ULTRA STRONG LAGER™ from his bag, cracked it open in a silent toast to Danny, then necked half of it – taking a sharp breath through his teeth before loudly expressing his satisfaction.

As the engined revved beneath him, the coach juddered irregularly into tooth-shaking life. Moments later they were pulling out of the garage and shooting straight down towards the motorway.

Bilko settled back again. This was gonna be fun.

*

'What the fuck...?' said Deb.

'Aye. Swot I said and all.' Sal were right pissed off.

They were both standing at the kitchen sink and looking out the window at the back yard beyond. Something had been through the fuckin' bins in the night.

'Probably a fox or sommat,' suggested Deb.

'Aye,' agreed Sal. 'Or a dog or sommat.'

'Bastard!' spat Deb. That were the last thing she fancied doing this afternoon, getting down on her hands and knees and clearing up the cartons of rotting milk and festering muck that were strewn across the concrete.

'Bugger it! Fuckin foxes!' snapped Sal.

'Where the fuckin bin bags then?' asked Deb.

'Oh aye. Don't spose you'd know would you. They're under here, in fuckin cupboard!'

Deb eyed the overflowing bin bag that sat in the corner of the kitchen, overflowing with cartons of rotting milk and festering muck. It looked liked Jabba the fuckin' Hutt. She laughed out loud.

'Ere!' said Sal, whose temper were getting worse by the minute. 'Woss so fuckin funny! I always put the fuckin rubbish out.'

'Ey, it looks like Jabba the fuckin Hutt does that!'

'Oh aye', said Sal, laughing at the bulging black bin liner despite her mate's sluttish ways. 'It does at that!'

'Come on then,' said Deb handing Sal one of the black bags. 'Let's fuckin' do it then.'

*

As the coach headed down towards Liverpool, Bilko looked at the rows of empty seats in front of him. There were only one or two others in the bus. And the hostess. He watched her sashaying up and down the aisle. He couldn't take his eyes off her shapely arse, which moved independently of the grey polyester uniform skirt. The name tag on her white National Express blouse told him that her name was Barbara and the blouse was sufficiently unbuttoned that when she bent down to ask Bilko if he wanted a cup of tea or a bag of crisps or owt he could see her tits. He pretended to think it over, asking automatic questions like 'What flavour crisps do you have?' They were pretty tanned. Almost golden. 'What cold drinks have you got?' Either she'd just come back from holiday or she went to one a them tanning shops. He imagined her taking off her clothes and undoing her bra before lying down naked on a sun bed. 'Have you got egg sarnies?' Rubbing sun tan lotion onto soft, warm skin. 'How much is tea?' They were vibrating gently from the motion of the coach. Completely mesmerising. 'No ta,' he'd said eventually, when there could be no further excuse for keeping her there. He wondered if she fancied him. If she'd been showing him her tits deliberately like.

When she'd gone back down to her seat at the front, he retrieved his can of ULTRA STRONG LAGER™ from where he'd stuffed it, and necked what was left. Then he settled back, closed his eyes for a second. But not for long cos suddenly he reached down to pull his bag out from under his feet, and plonked it on the empty seat next to him.

Suddenly fancying a fag, he reached into his parka pocket for the packet of Old Holborn and was puzzled not to find it there. It were a moment or two before he remembered that he'd treated hizself to a pack of Bennies. Or rather Danny had. He pulled off the cellophane and broke open the packet, flicking the bottom with his thumb in order to throw a tab up from the ranks. He pulled down the retractable ashtray in the back of the seat in front, then placing the incredibly fat-feeling fag in his gob he struck an acrid-smelling lucifer and sucked the smoke deep into his lungs. Outside the bus it started raining, and he watched the water forming gravity-defying streaks up the window; pooling in mercurial blobs on the sill.

The fag seemed to be gone before he'd lit it, Bilko's thoughts were racing that fast. He reluctantly stubbed it out in the seat-back asher, then turned to unzip his bag. As he rummaged amongst the clean T-shirts and other assorted contents his mind wandered back to the previous night.

It hadn't taken him long to rush round to Deb and thats' place. He'd trod carefully down the back way, counting along the houses until he came to their yard. As usual, as he'd hoped, there was a mountain of black bin bags next to the step. All manner of rotting milk cartons and assorted kinds of festering muck were spilling out of them. He was glad that the bin men hadn't been round yet, that would have made his life a lot more complicated. As he approached the rubbish sacks he could hear a scratching noise which seemed to emanate from deep within one of the bags. And even though he were treading quietly, the creature responsible must've sensed his presence, because the scratching stopped for a second, then a big brown shape appeared. It regarded him with a quizzical eye. Suddenly emboldened, Bilko smiled at his fellow creature of the night. Rats were clever, he knew that, and this one was obviously sizing up his newly-won occult credentials. Suddenly the rat bolted, dashing straight between his army surplus footwear. The rat was bigger than his boots, almost the size of a cat. Bilko practically jumped out of his skin, and had to fight the urge to throw up as he felt the prime specimen of Rattus Norvegicus brushing against his ankles. He took a deep breath, and stood still for a second or two. Trying to compose himself. Obviously the rat had sensed his power and was afraid. That was good then. It were a sign. Some kind of Omen. From the spirits probably. Confirmation of his ever-increasing powers of darkness. He could feel the spirits at his shoulders, guiding him. Let them come, he whispered, I ain't a-fuckin-fraid a them furry fuckers!

Steeling himself he crept over to the topmost sack. He tried to lift it up but as he did so the thin black plastic just ripped under the weight of the festering muck within, spilling its foul-smelling contents onto the concrete yard. For a second he cursed the poor quality of recycled British plastic goods, but then he realised that it would make his job easier if everything were spread out. How could it be any other way. He couldn't do it by feel alone. He squatted down and rummaged through the egg shells and the potato peelings. The empty cider bottles and the fag packets. No. There were nothing here. He tipped over the next bag, and started sorting the contents with the side of his boots. Same story; just a load of kitchen stuff and food cartons. Endless fag butts. This was no good. He couldn't use any of this shit. By the time he got to the fourth and final bag he were giving up hope of finding anything. But as he tipped it out he saw it – amongst the old tea bags and the empty baked bean tins – a small plastic carrier bag with its handles tied together. He had to stop himself from laughing out loud. It contained, as he knew it would, the contents of Deb's bathroom waste bin. He ripped it open and rummaged through the empty packs of hair dye and shampoo until he'd found what he was looking for.

Stuffing the treasures into his pockets he crept out to

the back street, quickly looked left and right to check that the coast was clear, then legged it.

Once he'd gone, and his footsteps no longer echoed off the backs of the terraced houses, the rat reappeared out of the U-bend of the now defunct outside-bog, sniffing the air and looking left and right to check that the coast was clear. Only this time it wasn't alone. Dozens of them poured out of every shadowy corner and, squeaking with delight, they began to feast on the decaying fruits of Deb's generosity.

'Wake up.'

Someone was jogging his shoulder.

'Uh?'

'Wake up! We're there.'

It were the stewardess. As he half-opened his eyes Bilko was greeted once again by the sight of her gorgeously tanned tits. He gawped at them in silence, pretending to still be asleep. As she joggled his shoulder again they wobbled back and forth. His cock was instantly straining against its cotton confines.

'Uh?' he said again, feigning sleepy befuddlement.

'Come on sleepyhead, wake up. We're there I...'

She suddenly stopped when she caught sight of the contours of the blood-filled love bone which was swelling the sleeping passenger's smart black levi's. Since she spent every day making small talk with a bunch of chain-smoking, yellow-haired coach drivers the sight of some young flesh seemed to flick a switch in her cunt, which instantly cried out for some cock action.

'I'm going up the canteen Barbara. Coming?' yelled the driver from the doorway.

'Aye. Be up in a minute,' she retorted to the by-pass patient-to-be.

They were parked round the back of the station now, cos they had a couple of hours off. As she'd waved off the two old biddies who'd been sitting at the front talking about their friends' operations, both she and the driver had forgotten all about the other passenger at the back. Now that the driver was gone though, she tiptoed down the aisle and flicked the switch which would lock the pneumatically-operated swing door.

As she sashayed up the aisle, her cunt seemed to get wetter and wetter with every step. By the time she reached the back seat, she knew that she'd not be able to sit still until she'd had a bone-shaking cum.

Thinking ahead, she drew the curtains by the back three rows of seats, then leaned over in front of the randy young passenger:

'Come on. Wake up!' she breathed.

'Uh? We there yet?' Bilko asked, opening his eyes.

'Not quite yet we're not,' she winked, unbuttoning her National Express issue blouse. He smelt of executive washroom soap, and she'd shagged in that many bus station showers that just the smell of it made her cunt quiver with excitement.

Bilko's eyes widened in astonishment, as he instantly assessed the situation. It was like a dream come true; the stewardess wanted some cock action and he was about to provide it. More than just willingly. She untucked her blouse and let it fall completely open, giving the well-dressed young occultist an unimpeded view of the objects of his desire.

'Like what you see then?' She cupped her hands beneath her tits.

'Aye. Sound.' Bilko nodded enthusiastically.

Slipping her fingers between silk and skin, she liberated her tits from their lacey supports. Bilko feasted his eyes on her big, dark nipples.

'Come on then!' she urgently exclaimed.

Bilko put his arms around her waist and pulled her bodily towards him. He ran his fingers up her waist and moments later he held a suntanned tit in each hand. He kissed her nipples greedily and sucked first one and then the other. They tasted like heaven and hell all mixed up together and that was a delicacy he couldn't get enough of. The randy stewardess moaned in delight. It'd been a while since anyone had made such a meal of her gorgeous tits. Bilko, meanwhile, was sucking so hard he had to keep remembering to breathe. He ran one hand down the 'in-flight' attendant's back bone, slipping it briefly under the polyester waistband of her uniform skirt. The more he sucked and lapped at her tits the wetter Barbara seemed to get, until, unable to restrain herself from her impending impalement she suddenly reached down, wriggled her hips, and yanked up her skirt with both hands. Bilko's hands, meanwhile, seemed to have a life of their own. He was still totally preoccupied with the tits in his gob, but his hands had already encountered the smooth warm skin of her arse. They'd already figured out that she wasn't wearing any knickers, and found the suspenders with which her stockings were kept up. He slipped a couple of fingers straight into her creamy cunt, feeling her shudder with delight as he did so. Suddenly aware of his aching loins he quickly licked the cunt juice off his fingers then undid his button fly and liberated his cock from within the bounds of decency. Then he pulled Barbara on top of him, so that her stockinged knees were planted firmly on the seats either side of him. He could feel her hairy bush tickling the tip of his cock, which was as hard and shiney as a pebble worn smooth by countless centuries in the ocean. With a gasp she fell onto his cock. 'I wanna ride you to hell and back you randy bastard!' she shouted as she impaled herself on the blood filled love bone and, as if in reply, he drove it repeatedly through the hot, pulsating heart of her being. Bilko felt the walls of the underworld closing in on him as Barbara bucked and howled above him like a banshee bitch on heat. As they jointly reached their Darwinian destination, the sights and sounds of the National Express coach interior melted away, only to be replaced by a Bosch-like landscape of decadent and twisted desire; an empire of ungodly gratification. Barbara and Bilko had created a Garden of Earthly Delights and, as he shot what seemed like gallons of hot spunk into her convulsing cunt, they saw that it was good

XV

London Daily News
Monday October 20th 1999

STOP! IN THE NAME OF GOD
'ONWARD CHRISTIAN SOLDIERS' CALL TO LAUNCH 'SATANIC' FESTIVAL PROTEST

The Reverend Jeremiah Jones, charismatic leader of the London-based Church of the Everlasting Day, today launched a nationwide Christian coalition 'army' to fight against the influence of 'Satanic Rock Music' in general, and more particularly an up-coming pop festival which is dedicated, he says, to furthering the forces of darkness.

In a press conference held at the London Methodist Centre in Westminster, Jones (53) begged all churchgoers in the country to join the protest. He spoke eloquently of the threat to the Nation's children that is posed by the so-called 'Death Metal' cult, and the need for Christians of all denominations to 'stand firm against this evil in the name of our Lord Jesus Christ'.

While a choir sang the well known hymn 'Onward Christian Soldiers', the strikingly-featured albino Church Leader laid out his plans for the protest. Firstly he urged that concerned Christians should write to the Archbishop of Canterbury, then he announced a 'Million Man March' – modelled on the famous Washington DC protest held by the Nation of Islam and other African American groups – which he hoped would prevent the festival going ahead by sheer force of numbers.

London Daily News reporters attempted to contact the reclusive organisers of the 'Festival of Night', which is to be held in historical Whitby on Halloween night, but were unable to speak with any of their representatives.

TURN TO PAGE 5

XVI

Deb couldn't believe her ears. Pete had arrived back in town after his London jaunt, lugging flight cases and gaffa tape for the Sisters. As soon as he'd walked into the living room of Deb and that's place, he'd reached into his jacket pocket with a flourish worthy of a magician and produced three laminated black passes for the Festival of Night. The magic words 'Access all areas' were printed across the front, beneath the gothic script of the festival logo. They were dead cool, and Deb was gobsmacked. 'Ta!' was all she could say. 'Aye, it's sound is that,' Tish added. 'Ta very much!' Then Pete had checked the Austin Osman Spare photocopied mural on the wall, and the skull on the mantlepiece.

'Wow!' he'd said. 'Zit real d'you think!'

'What d'yer mean. You should fuckin know!'

'How's that then?' Pete's brow furrowed.

'Well it were you what give it me. Wern it?'

'I think I'd remember sommat like that!' said Pete laughing. 'It's fuckin sound though. It is real intit!'

'Aye, I reckon it is. Fuck. I thought it were you that give it me.'

Deb was parroting now, her mouth operating independently of her brain. Inside she was re-assessing her innermost thoughts. If it wern't Pete what give it to her then who was it. There was only one answer, but her brain wouldn't allow her to think it. It were Tish what gave voice to the inescapable conclusion that Deb was resisting.

'It were fuckin Bilko! Ang on a sec!' Tish suddenly rushed from the room.

'Well,' said Deb, not wanting to piss Pete off too much. 'Who-ever it were it's fuckin sound intit!'

'Aye. It is at that,' said Pete, mentally computing the obvious fact that he had a rival for Deb's affections. He were glad that he'd come with some offerings of his own. 'You've got an admirer then, Deb?'

Deb couldn't help but look over at the 'access all areas' passes on the table...

'Aye mebbe I have. But I'm not interested in that twat.'

Pete breathed a mental sigh of relief. Thank fucking Christ for that. The whole week he'd been away he'd not thought of much else but the various imaginative ways he'd fuck the gorgeous goth bird when he got back. And now he was back, she looked more fuckable than ever. More than that: with her lank black hair and pale-white powdered face, them big black shadows round her eyes, her tattoos, her ripped up fishnets, her victorian whale bone corset and her junkshop Whitby Jet jewellery she looked totally fucking wicked.

Tish came back into the room brandishing last week's local paper.

'Eh!' she screeched. 'D'you reckon it were Bilko what done this then?'

'What?' Deb turned to see what her big-boned mate were going on about.

'This,' said Tish jabbing her finger at the front page of the paper.

Deb gulped when she read the headline: 'Leeds grave robbed'. She looked again at the skull on the mantelpiece. It looked like it were laughing at her. In her mind's eye she had visions of Bilko shovelling down into the soft earth and suddenly appearing with a putrefying skull, then holding it aloft in triumph.

Pete broke the ice.

'Well if it were him, he's done a fuckin good job a cleanin it up!'

Deb looked pale. She felt like she were gonna throw up. She couldn't look at the skull now without seeing the rotting flesh hanging off it in strips, the worms and the hair all messed up together. She'd heard a story about some Psychic Youths in Newcastle robbing graves so they could make Tibetan thigh bone trumpets a few year ago, they'd been caught and all. But the thought of someone robbing a fuckin grave in Leeds just to win her affections: it made her sick! Pete noticed the sudden change in her complexion; instead of being merely white, the gorgeous goth girl had gone a strange shade of green.

'Ang on,' he said, rummaging through his ruck sack. 'You look like you could use some of this!'

He pulled out an unopened bottle of Jack Daniels. He'd planned on saving it for when him and his mates were watching the footie at the weekend, but suddenly thought better of that particular plan.

'Here y'are then.' Tish produced a jumble-sale assortment of shot glasses out of what seemed like thin air.

When they'd drunk a few reckless toasts to the spirit of the violated corpse on the mantlepiece, Pete got some more skins out of his pocket and began to stick them together in the time-honoured fashion. Then he nicked one of Deb's Black Sobranies and began to roll a joint. Minutes later he was striking a lucifer which he flicked into the fireplace once it had done its job. After blowing out the flame which bloomed momentarily on the end of the spliff, he drew the powerful smoke deep into his lungs. Thanks to the skill of the famous Tennessee distillery Deb had mellowed a bit now: the charcoal filtering, the generations-old know-how and the un-hurried, ten year ageing process seemed to produce a similarly laid back attitude in the goth bird's previously freaked out brain.

'Za bit of a nutter then,' he stated, matter-of-factly. 'This Bilko character.'

'Aye I reckon he is.' Deb was in the act of pouring herself yet another measure of the smokey-flavoured whisky. She gulped it down like it were mother's milk.

She related the story of Bilko appearing at the Hell Fire Club with his new tats. Pete were laughing when she said, 'It's not even like he'd just got one done! On iz arm or sommat! He'd bloody done the lot! All over!'

'Not much of a fuckin Valentine izit! He's got it bad I

reckon,' said Tish. 'Jesus fuck! I mean, first he robs a grave, then he goes and gets the entire works of Austin Osman Spare tattooed on his body! What's he gonna think of next!'

'Aye,' said Deb. 'Thass what I'm a-fuckin-fraid of.'

She grabbed the joint which Pete were waving in her direction and sucked on it greedily. Inexplicably though, an image of Bilko suddenly popped into her mind. It was accompanied by a sharp twinge in her cunt, and a sudden feeling of wetness. She squirmed, frowned, then put it down to Pete's proximity and her desire to have him fuck her senseless before the witching hour was up. She leaned over and kissed her roady lover, long and deep, then nibbled his ear and whispered:

'I can't wait to fuck you, you randy bastard.'

*

Bilko legged it through the night, gulping the cold air into his lungs as he went. He ran onto the station platform and boarded the Sprinter train just as the doors hissed shut. Plonking his bag down on the seat opposite, he chuckled to himself, then got comfortable. He'd be back in Liverpool before the witching hour, then he could make the sleeper connection up to Glasgow in comfort. It weren't bad, this travelling business. He'd always thought that his various mates who'd gone of to Goa or where-ever were sad fucks who were looking for sommat they'd never find, whether they were doing the looking in Armley or Afghanistan. All that shit about travelling for its own sake, and 'I'm not a tourist' and 'meeting real people, man' was bullshit as far as he were concerned. He'd broadened his mind without leaving his flat practically. Just by acknowledging the ancient powers of the spirits, and letting them into his life. No, the best kind of travelling was when you did it for a reason, he decided. Travelling with a purpose, that were where it were at.

In the distance, even above the racket of the train wheels' rhythmic clackety-clacking, he could hear the sound of sirens rushing through the night. It had worked! He stood up and shut the window.

Fishing a Walkman out of the parka's capacious pockets he pushed the phones into his ears and pressed play, then banged out an imaginary chord as the howling guitar intro to Sacreligious kicked in. Moments later a discordant bass pumped up the volume before Vlad Vargstrom's demonic vocal began to shriek across the desolate landscape of sound, conjuring up the image of angry and vengeful Norse gods racing like supernatural wolves across a primitive Europe and extinguishing the flames of hope. Settling back as best he could in the sprinter's uncomfortable plastic seat, Bilko hummed along atonaly with Vargstrom's Swedish-inflected stream of vicious vocal vitriol.

*

As the horny black-garbed goth bird stuck a finger up his arse, Pete took a sharp intake of breath through his teeth before expressing his satisfaction. All thoughts of Bilko had been banished by several hours of mellow chat, half a bottle of Jack Daniels, and a few joints of Pete's best black. Now Deb's fat friend had gone to bed and they'd retired to bed and all. Deb had wasted no time in getting Pete's kit off, and the sight of her deft and boney fingers unbuttoning his leathers had been like visual viagra to the sex-starved roady, producing an instant hard-on. Their hungry mouths found each other and they kissed long and deep. Then he slipped one hand up her skirt, carressing her stockinged thighs until he encountered the hot, wet entrance to hell, while his other hand snaked down the front of her dress and began to caress her tits. When he lightly pinched one of her nipples it seemed to flick a switch in Deb's cunt and she suddenly squirmed with the instant heat of her diabolical desires.

Pete unclasped the fiddly fastenings of her antique silk bodice with the seasoned touch of the professional and as he sucked on her newly liberated tits Deb reacted like a creature possessed, sinking her teeth into his neck and sucking till she could taste the bruise, while simultaneously slipping another digit up his hairy shit hole.

'Suck my cock!' he pleaded.

'Bugger that!' said Deb, cos though she was a right randy bitch she never sucked cock. In a matter of seconds she'd yanked both fingers out of his shit chute, pushed him down onto the bed and gathered up her skirts about her before straddling him. The sight of the gorgeous goth towering above him only hardened Pete's resolve to give her the most bone-shaking cum imaginable as she grabbed his veiny cock with her delicate fist and guided it to the hairy gates of hades.

'I wanna ride you to hell and back you randy bastard!' she shouted as she impaled herself on his blood-filled love bone and, as if in reply, he drove it unerringly through the hot, pulsating heart of her being. As they fornicated fiendishly, Pete felt the walls of the underworld closing in on him, and Deb was bucking and howling above him like a banshee bitch on heat. As Deb's thighs began to shudder uncontrollably the sights and sounds of her bedroom melted away, only to be replaced by a Bosch-like landscape of decadent and twisted desire; an empire of ungodly gratification populated by a host of horny demons and other unnatural creatures all completely unbounded by the laws of nature. Deb and Pete had created a grotesque and gratuitous Garden of Earthly Delights and, as he shot what seemed like gallons of hot spunk into her convulsing cunt, they saw that it was good.

*

Bilko couldn't believe his luck. It was a dry and windless night, and The Church of Scotland Parish Church of St. Aloysius, Burns Road, Moffat, was not only well screened by trees, it seemed to be made almost entirely of wood.

He'd confidently bought a can of petrol at a garage on the other side of town, exchanging a bit of 'bloody-British-cars-can't-take-the fuckers-anywhere'-type banter with the assistant by way of explanation. He were right glad of the change of image - not only had it landed him the instant shag with Barbara on the coach, but it made him look like a regular-to-successful kind of guy. The kind of guy that no-one - randy stewardesses with a penchant for on-board sex excepted - would take a second glance at.

Pacing slowly round the church he carefully splashed the petrol onto various strategic parts of the woodwork, then ran a trail of it along the sheltered edge of the stone path. He chucked the empty petrol can through the cracked stone of an ivy covered tomb, then took a candle out of his pocket. Moving out of range of the dangerously inflammable vapour he melted the wax on the base of the candle and stuck it onto a packet of swan vestas, before lighting the wick with one of the red-topped lucifers. The system had worked pretty well at Pwlheli, there were no reason why it shouldn't be equally destructive here. Shielding the flame with his hand, he advanced slowly towards the church. He chuckled at the sudden vision of himself as an altar boy carrying one a them big brass candle sticks in procession down the aisle, then cursed as he realised that his stifled snort had still been sufficient to blow out the tiny yellow flame. He re-lit it, remembering the way that the Welsh church had caught fire, remembering the tongues of flame which wreaked such uncontrollable devastation. It were a right shame that he couldn't stick around to watch the show. Probably could have blended into the crowd, but as a stranger he might have drawn a bit of attention to himself, and that weren't the point. Plus he vaguely remembered sommat about arsonists often hanging about to watch the flaming fruits of their fire-starting handiwork, and he weren't no common or garden arsonist: he was doing the Devil's work on Earth, and out to shag Deb senseless. The prospct of getting banged up as a petty villain making an anti-social 'cry for help' was not only an offense to his pride, it would well and truly fuck the grand plan to boot.

As soon as the sputtering candle were set down on the

path, he arranged a horse-shoe of bricks around it, to shelter it from any freakish gust of wind, then turned briskly away and walked through the woods towards the small Scottish town's small Scottish railway station. The candle would take about ten minutes to burn down, and there was an early morning 'milk train' due to make a stop in Moffat about ten minutes from now; he'd be half way back to Glasgow before the fire had even started.

Four down, he thought to himself. Four down and one to go. Derby and Belfast had been first, and now, thanks to no-fucking-body but him, Pwlheli and Moffat had been added to the list. He didn't know who'd started the first two fires, didn't matter any road. What did matter was that he, Bilko, had seen the patterns. Thanks to the spirits' interventions he'd seen what had to be done. He'd seen the pentagram of fire being drawn across the British Isles, and he knew – 'Give and ye shall get', the spirits had told him – that completing the profane symbol would bring him the full support of the forces of darkness and the power to make sure that the second part of his plan to fuck the shit out of Deb could work.

Four down, he grinned to himself again. That just left Whitby.

Deb and that had been talking about some fucking great abbey or sommat, and Whitby were the last point of the degraded diagram he was drawing across the land. He'd complete the evil image by torching this fucking abbey, then the powers of darkness would be harnessed in his quest for Deb's cunt. He longed to see the historical house of God going up in flames, collapsing in on itself, until there was nothing left but a smoldering ruin. What a spectucular fucking finale to his nefarious plans that would be, especially if he was riding the horny goth bird to hell and back while it burned.

XVII

The make-up artist paused for a second. She didn't know what to do and she had until about yesterday to decide. Sprucing up the guests for TV interviews was normally a matter of applying some thick panstick to make sure that they didn't look like walking corpses, but the interviewee who sat before her now was unlike anything she'd ever had to deal with.

'What's wrong young lady?'

'Nothing, just....'

'Have you been baptised in the name of the Lord?'

'No! I... er, yes. Yes I have as a matter of fact.'

She quickly decided to apply a pale white powderwhich would, if nothing else, take the shine off the pallid preacherman's face. There was no point giving him a normal looking complexion; probably better if he looked as unearthly as possible. The glare off his snow white features would give the cameramen a headache, but that wasn't her problem. She quickly finished the job and retired from the set as the outside broadcast which was playing off the studio monitors drew to a close:

'Ironically,', veteran BBC Scottish Correspondent Martin Dixon successfully stifled his schadenfreude-induced mirth. 'The arsonist or arsonists didn't actually start the fire. It was the pipe-smoking Reverand James MacDonald who inadvertantly set the church ablaze when he threw away a smouldering match as he went to unlock the church this morning. A spokesman from Motherwell Royal Infirmary has confirmed that the Reverand MacDonald has suffered twenty degree burns, and that his condition is currently critical.'

'And....cue Jimmy!'

The tinny voice in his ear was all the encouragement that James Bovrelle needed. He was well known, both in the trade and around the living rooms of Britain, as a supercillious twat with a distinctive line in arrogant, public school disdain, and knew the producer was trying to wind him up by using the diminutive form of his name. He grimaced, looking for all the world like he was having a huge shit: I wouldn't get this kind of treatment with the other bloody lot, he thought to himself. He addressed the camera then turned to the latest in a long line of freakish guests who he'd been called upon to interview in his long career on BBC current affairs flagship The News Review:

'I'm joined in the studio by Jeremiah Jones, charismatic leader of the Church of the Everlasting Day. Mr Jones, you've recently launched a campaign against so-called Death Metal music. It's well known that certain adherants to that, er, musical cult have been responsible for burning down churches in,' Bovrelle's features pinched disdainfully, 'Noooorway... Is that really what we're seeing here?'

Jeremiah Jones was no fool when it came to free publicity. He knew that launching into evangelical gobbledegook now would alienate precisely the middle-English Christian scum that he needed to swell the numbers of his march. Coming on all 'fire and brimstone' would do nothing to help him fight the good fight now. To this end he'd already decided to come across as the voice of reasonable concern.

'Thank you, James. Yes, I regret to say that that's exactly what we're seeing here: how many more honest men of God will have to be martyred before the good people of England stand up and say 'enough!' And let's get one thing straight: we're all reasonable people. I'm not one of these fringe nutters who think that if you play some popular beat disc backwards you'll hear a message from the Devil. But this music actually does champion satanic beliefs, that is its purpose, and it does it in such a way that can only harm the minds of impressionable young people. For example there's a long playing record at number ten in this week's album charts which actually contains the instruction 'Burn their stinking churches down'. The message couldn't be clearer than that. And now person or persons unknown are putting these vile ideas into practice.'

'You are focusing your campaign on the so-called 'Festival of Night' pop festival which is taking place in Whitby on Halloween are you not?'

'I am indeed, James. Now I'm a great believer not only in the love of God and the fellowship of the Holy Spirit, but also in this great democracy of ours. Free speech is a wonderful thing. But surely to give a platform to groups who advocate actual violence, and I stress that, who advocate actual violence against the very bedrock of our civilisation, is going one step too far. The Home Secretary has to act before this despicable cult goes any further...'

Bovrelle noticed the producer giving the 'wind up' signal.

'I'm afraid...' he started to say, but Jones was not in the mood for being wound up before he'd finished saying his piece, and simply turned up the volume:

'That is why I would urge Christian people all over the country...'

'...that's all that...'

'...to join our crusade...'

'...we have...'

'...and show exactly how we feel about this filth.'

'...time for...'

'The next church to burn down,' Jones looked directly at the camera. 'Could be yours. Let's join together and stop this happening!'

Bovrelle breathed a sigh of relief. The producer was frantically making the throat cut gesture which meant 'shut the fucker up' to those in the know.

'Thankyou very much Mr. Jones. And we asked the organisers of the 'Festival of Night' to appear on the show, but they declined to be interviewed. Moving on, we just have time to look at tomorrow's front pages...'

Jeremiah Jones was ushered quickly off the set by an earnest and fresh-faced young production assistant.

'Thank you very much for coming in at such short notice Mr Jones. There's a driver waiting for you in reception. I must say, I thought you were very reasonable,' the PA gushed. 'I wish you the best of luck with your crusade.'

Jones was always on the look-out for potential congregation fodder, especially of the young and fresh-faced variety. He turned to the Oxbridge graduate:

'Tell me something young man. Have you been baptised in the holy waters of the River Jordan?'

'Yes I... well, actually no.' The confession made the well-presented PA blush.

Jones put a fatherly hand on the young man's shoulder.

'You are always welcome in the house of God my son. We have daily services!'

'Th-thank you. Yes, m-m-maybe I'll do that. Thank you.'

'Peace be with you child!' Jones squeezed the new recruit's shoulder and beamed.

As he got into the lavishly upholstered car Jones chuckled to himself. He could well understand why the festival organisers hadn't wished to appear on the show as well! They'd never do that. Not in a million years!

He laughed out loud.

The driver looked at the freakish man of God in his rear view mirror for a second before putting his foot down and tooling out of the BBC TV Centre carpark.

XVIII

Deb got up and turned off the telly. They'd all been pissing themselves at the religious posturing of the weird albino on the News Review, confident that nothing the pallid preacher could do would stop their fun at the forthcoming Festival of Night. Pete and that, along with all the other crew, had digs sorted out in the middle of Whitby and he'd said they'd be welcome to stay. They'd all booked their seats on the National Express coach to Scarborough, and then it were just a half hour bus ride to Whitby. Despite herself, she couldn't fuckin' wait. She'd been to that many festivals that it weren't a big deal or owt. But something told her that this one were gonna be totally fuckin sound.

Luckily Bilko hadn't shown his face recently. In fact no-one had seen him at all. Ron had been getting right pissed off about that, said Bilko owed him money, and where was the conniving cunt. Deb couldn't help him, was glad to have shot of the bug-eyed dealer's persistant and mis-guided attentions and that were that. Funny thing was – and she were keeping this to herself – that he kept popping into her mind. Completely unbidden and at the strangest times. She'd suddenly see his leering fizzog in her minds eye, and feel her cunt twitching hotly at the same time. Ugh! Surely she wasn't starting to fancy him. Perhaps she was coming down with cystitis or sommat. Aye, that were probably it.

*

Bilko was standing in front of the mirror in the grotty B&B where he'd holed up for a day or three. He'd toyed with the idea of sending Danny a postcard, but Barrow was such a shit hole that there weren't any for sale in the local newsies. Probably just as well.

Barrow - for fuck's sake! He wasn't sure why he'd chosen the place. Once he'd got to Glasgow he'd been pleased to discover that there was plenty of dough left in the kitty: more than enough to just lie low for a couple of days. And when the train back to Leeds via Doncaster had pulled in at the northern seaside town's dismal little railway station, something about the godforsaken place had appealed to him. On the spur of the moment he'd just grabbed his bag and hopped smartly off the train.

As he strolled down the hill towards the town centre he'd felt more relaxed than he had in ages. No, more than just relaxed. He'd felt positively powerful. That were it. It were the sense of well being that came with making things happen your own way, by any means necessary. He didn't know whether to pity the pathetic specimens of human life that paraded past him, or just to toy with the sad little pawns then grind them under heel and laugh in their miserable impotent faces.

It hadn't taken him long to find a B&B with vacancies. They were all desperate for business, and looking around at the place it were no fucking wonder.

He'd stripped down to his keks now, and was admiring his new tats in the dressing table mirror. Standing full on, then sideways, then craning his neck over his shoulder at the ones on his back. He couldn't help but stare at the plethora of inky faces which covered his body, mesmerised by the unearthly fizzogs which seemed to move and blur before his eyes, shifting in and out of focus almost as if they really were unearthly creatures and desperate spirits which had been summoned from the other side by Pete Panther's buzzing needle. They wouldn't have seemed any more real if they'd started moaning eerily and wailing out their centuries of anguish. That Pete Panther's a fucking star, he thought to himself. A fucking star.

He moved over to the bed, squeezing his balls through his new dugs with one hand. Just a matter of time till Deb were his and his alone, he couldn't fucking wait. His bag was on the bed. Opening it up he reached in and took out a box which was wrapped up in T-shirts for safe-keeping. He laid down on top of the covers and took off the lid, then carefully picked through the bog roll inside and pulled out the doll.

Well 'doll' would be overstating things a little. The crudely fashioned wax figure was little more than a big hunk of melted candles from which five stumps protruded. One of the stumps, the one which stuck out of the end, had a face roughly drawn on it - it looked like a child's drawing only worse, but considering that it had been done with the stub-end of a lipstick he'd got out of Deb's dustbin Bilko was pretty pleased with the result. There was a ball of messy black hair what she must have pulled out of her hair brush, and that was kind of half-visible through the wax of the diabolical Deb-doll's head. Wrapped around the 'body' and sort of half-melted into the wax was a kind of black, lacy garment. Bilko pulled the front of this lacy garment out with his little finger and fiddled with the two lip-stick blobs thus revealed. The lacy clothing was in fact a pair of Deb's old knickers which, again, had come out of her dustbin. He lifted the doll close to his face and took a long, deep sniff. They smelt of heaven and hell all mixed up together. Up-ending the waxy form he inspected a ragged gash which he'd carved between the two leg stumps. Protruding from this candle-wax-cunt was a piece of string. It was out of sight now, but in the centre of the frightful figurine, buried deep in its waxy heart, was one of Deb's used tampons – there had even been a pubic hair stuck in the encrusted menstrual blood. The detail, he thought to himself smugly. It's all in the detail. That little carrier bag of stuff from Deb's bathroom wastebasket had been an occultist's treasure trove. It had divulged all of these intimate delights, and now that they'd been incorporated into this effigy of the sexy goth bird, Bilko knew – cos the spirits had told him – that this was more than just a doll; that in some strange and mysterious way this devil-doll was Deb and that his power over her could only increase until she became about as capable of resisting his innermost desires as this diabolical mannikin.

He smiled to himself, then gently tickled the crudely

carved gash, tugging occasionally on the tampon string. This was giving him a hard on. The thought that wherever she was, Deb's cunt would now be hot and quivering and desperate for several inches of Bilko's blood-filled love bone was a right fuckin turn on, and he didn't need the spirits to tell him that.

There was a knock at the door. Bilko stopped fondling his cock for a sec and looked up:

'Who is it?'

'It's me; Mrs Blackley.'

'Hang on!'

What the fuck did she want? Bilko carefully placed the deb-doll back in its box then grabbed a T-shirt, pulling it over his head as he walked to the door and opened it.

'Hello Mr. Spare. I were just wondering if you'd be stayin' for... Sorry I, er...'

The glamorous landlady's sentence trailed off as she caught sight of the bulge in Bilko's clean cotton kecks.

Bilko sensed the source of her discomfiture and decided to play it to his advantage. He could tell that the randy landlady was desperate to impale herself on his blood-filled love bone. He opened the door fully, to give her a better view.

'Come in Mrs B.'

Mrs B didn't need any further encouragement, she shut the door behind her and immediately started to unbutton her flatteringly-cut housecoat. She's not bad looking, Bilko thought to himself, and the sight of her enormous tits made his cock throb and twitch at the prospect of shagging her senseless. Mrs B stuck her tongue down his throat; her husband were out at work, and it'd been ages since she'd got on her knees to suck off some young cock.

What Bilko didn't realise, as he sucked hungrily on his landlady's big, dark and rapidly-hardening nipples, was that his stopping in Barrow was anything but an accident. As she got down on her knees and began sucking on his veiny cock he was probably too preoccupied to care that the sleepy seaside town he thought he'd selected at random was in fact set in the exact centre of the demonic diagram which he'd been helping to create. And far from being the architect of the devilish plans which were underfoot, he was little more than the hired-in labour.

But Bilko was not to know that. He'd find it out, the hard way, in a couple of days, but not just yet. So let's leave him with his little fantasies for a while longer and let him shag Mrs B in peace.

IXX

'Onward Christian So-ho-ho-holdiers,
Marching as to-o war.
With the Cross of Jesus,
Going on before!'

The Christians were in good spirits. The Church of the
Everlasting Day was packed into a mini-convoy of coaches
which itself headed up a much bigger convoy from all over the
country which had converged on the M1 at Leeds and now – as
it crossed the North Yorkshire Moors on its way to Robin
Hood's Bay – stretched as far as the eye could see: almost a
thousand coaches were speeding through the crisp autumn
morning. The sun was shining on the rolling miles of gorse and
heather which was just beginning to turn brown, sheep and birds
scattered from the roadside in alarm as the leading coach
ploughed on towards the sleepy seaside town from whence they
would begin their cliff-top march on Whitby.

Jeremiah Jones stood at the front of this coach, leading
his soldiers into war. He gazed out of the window, first at the
beauty of God's work, then at the endless stream of coaches
coming up behind. He picked up the microphone and lead his
disciples in the next hymn:

'All things bright and beautiful...' he began.

'ALL CREATURES GREAT AND SMALL,'
came the joyful response from his white-robed acolytes.

The Welshman was elated. The response to his modest
campaign – little more than a press conference and that
appearance on the News Review – had far surpassed even his
most wildly ambitious expectations, and now the good people
of England had come together to stand against the forces of
evil. The fact that he himself was also responsible for the single
largest gathering of so-called 'Death Metal' and 'goth' bands

only contributed to his sense of righteousness. Simply by setting up an off-the-peg, off-shore 'rock promotions' company, he'd managed to use the venality of the music business against itself. With the unheard of appearance fees 'Night Inc.' had offered for the Festival of Night, Jones had ensured that the massed ranks of satanic songsters were willing participants in their own undoing. They were falling over themselves to appear in the festival! Like lambs, - he thought to himself smugly - like lambs to the slaughter!

*

Deb, Tish and Sal joined the black-garbed throng which wound its way up Whitby's famous steps. The slabs of stone hugged every contour of the steep hill, almost a cliff, from the harbour below to the Abbey above; their surfaces eroded by both weather and centuries of human traffic. They could hear the PA warming up: gusts of sound booming over the crest above them. It was a motley collection of goths, and metal fans that trudged up those hundred steps. Deb and that were done up as usual; with their tattoos and ripped up fishnets, their victorian whale bone corsets and their junkshop Whitby Jet jewellery they looked totally fucking wicked. In front of them were some androgynous looking Marilyn Manson fans, and behind them some old rockers with Motorhead T-shirts. One emaciated goth peeled off his Neph T-shirt to reveal the tattoo on his back: '𝕿𝖍𝖊 𝕯𝖊𝖆𝖙𝖍 𝖔𝖋 𝕮𝖎𝖛𝖎𝖑𝖎𝖘𝖆𝖙𝖎𝖔𝖓 𝖎𝖘 𝖙𝖍𝖊 𝕱𝖚𝖙𝖚𝖗𝖊 𝖔𝖋 𝕽𝖔𝖈𝖐 'n' 𝕽𝖔𝖑𝖑', it said, in a blueing, gothic script.

Looking backwards and above the old rockers' heads for a second, Deb took in the sights of the sleepy harbour town. The bright autumn sunshine and the clear air brought the village into sharp focus. It were hard to believe that this were where Captain Cook had set sail from, that the biggest whaling fleets in Europe had once operated out of this village. On the crest of the hill that rose up on the other side of the harbour though, she could see the enormous whalebone arch which stood in silent testament to those days. For a second she tried to imagine what the place must've looked like; the ships crowding into the harbour; the promenading whores; the enormous carcasses being hacked up on the quaysides; the noise of the sailors roaring from tavern to tavern; the brawling and the boasting spilling off the boats and onto the narrow streets... but she couldn't.

*

Lakeland Times
Friday October 29th 1999

LANDLADY MURDERED - LOCAL SHOCK AT B&B SEX KILLING

Popular Barrow landlady, Mrs. Jemimah Blackley, was yesterday found brutally raped and murdered in her own guest house. A man was arrested last night in connection with the murder, and is currently helping Police with their enquiries.

A spokesman for the Lake District Retropolitan Police Force said: 'This murder was particularly brutal, and almost ritualistic in nature. Mrs Blackley was a popular local figure, and I can assure you that the officers in my command will not rest until we have a conviction. We don't at this point in time have reason to believe that other members of the public are at risk, but we would urge anyone who might have seen anything unusual at the Blackley Towers guest house to come forward and speak to us in the strictest confidence. I can assure the public that if they do come forward with information they will not be 'fitted up' with convenient unsolved local crimes - even if they are mentally ill.'

A neighbour of the Blackley's reflected the shock of the whole community last night: 'We just can't believe that something like this could happen here. She was a 'popular figure' in the area, and we're just frankly stunned!'

FULL STORY AND PICTURES ON PAGE 5

*

Vlad Vargstrom shivered and pulled his expensive Swedish over-coat around his shoulders. Despite the sun he was freezing cold. He was starting to regret the well laid plans for their appearance at the Festival of Night. It had seemed like a good idea at the time – to recreate the voyage of Count Dracula, on board a spectral tall ship and to arrive in Whitby with flaming torches and lead a macabre procession up the steps from the harbour and onto the festival stage in time for their headlining act – but now, after a night riding the choppy swell of the North Sea, a night in which the raging wind had whistled in the rigging and cut through to his very bones, he was wondering if it was all worth the hassle. Jorgenson and his music biz cronies were by now comfortably esconced in the nearest Holiday Inn, and Vargstrom was feeling decidedly jealous. He wondered if the Dogs' chainsmoking manager had been entirely truthful when he'd assured them that there were no tall ships to be had in England for love nor money, and that the only option was to hire the Gothenburg Princess for a week to make the round trip.

'Is more authentic,' Jorgenson had said, playfully slapping him on the back, 'If you guys actually travel on the ship as well. Think of the press coverage, yah!'

Well, perhaps. But now, looking up at the sails which hung limply from the masts, Vargstrom was starting to wonder if they'd even get to fucking Whitby.

Suddenly and without warning, the ship was surrounded by fog. Vargstrom hadn't noticed it approaching. He cursed the damp air and reached for his inhaler, this kind of weather played havoc with his asthma. There was still no wind, the sails were doing little more than fluttering uselessly from their stays, but Vargstrom had the definite impression of forward motion.

'Ah well,' he thought to himself as he stepped down below decks. 'Maybe we're getting somewhere after all.'

'Religion is the new Rock 'n' Roll!'

Jeremiah Jones's voice boomed through the PA which was set up at the cliff top carpark where coach after coach was spilling forth its Christian cargo. Some coaches had had to park miles back down the road, and the happy-clappy protestors were, even as he spoke, beginning their march. People would still be arriving in Robin Hoods Bay when he was in Whitby he reflected. It was going to be a continuous stream of pure belief that no amount of unbelievers could stop. They would swamp the forces of darkness by sheer force of numbers.

'The meek shall inherit the Earth!' he announced joyfully. 'Especially when there's this many of us!'.

He surveyed the crowd of Christians which stretched over the hillside before him. All were basking in the one true light, happy to be of service to the Good Fight which must now be fought. In a moment, banners and white robes fluttering in the breeze, the Church of the Everlasting Day would lead the faithful multitudes along the cliff top path to Whitby, and salvation.

He handed the microphone over to the Bishop of Bexhill-on-Sea, then stepped down off the platform to find his attractive blonde PA. Catching his eye in the crowd the Welshman beckoned him over.

'Where's my sun-block, child?' he asked.

*

'Woss that then?' yelled Deb above the noise of the gargantuan Festival of Night PA system, pointing through the ruins of the abbey at a huge white stage which had been set up in the next field.

'Beer tent probly!' said Tish.

The Christian Cocksuckers were playing on stage, and

the dark sounds they conjured from their instruments seemed slightly at odds with the glorious, sunny weather, but that did nothing to dampen the enthusiasm of the dark hordes who were spread out in front of the stage. Deb and that were somewhere between the mosh pit at the front and the supine forms of stoned gothdom that littered the grass around the edge of the crowd.

'This one's called 'The Virgin Mary takes it up the arse'!' boomed the Suckers' vocalist. His voice was quickly subsumed by the noise generated by the rest of the band, becoming an almost inaudible component of the general sonic assault. The sounds of thousands of Christian hymn-singers in the next field were ever present; phased and modified by wind and distance. To Deb and that it sounded like the Suckers were running some kind of Gregorian sample through the whole of their set; weird and other-worldly hymn singing that only served to amplify the evil sound for which they musically strove.

'Eh! Thass sound is that!' screeched Sal.

'Aye,' Deb confirmed. 'Sounds a bit like Psychic TV duntit!'

'What?'

'Like Psychic TV,' repeated Deb, turning up the volume. 'No s'Cocksuckers intit!'

'Sounds like Psychic TV though! That chanting!'

'What?'

'Chanting!'

'Oh aye!' agreed Sal.

'They're dis-fuckin-gustin!' Tish'd finally got back from the bogs. 'Sin anybody yet?'

Deb winced. Her cystitis was killing her. She made her excuses, unheard, and hurried off to the bog to piss for the umpteenth time that afternoon. The weird thing was that she also felt a bit pre-menstrual. Like she were just about to come on. She were that anorexic that she'd not had a period in about three years, so hadn't thought to pack any tampons. Just my fucking luck, she thought, as she pushed through the crowds;

here I am stuck in a field with a fucking itchy cunt, a permanent desire to piss myself, about to fucking come on and there's not a fucking tampon machine in fucking sight!

*

Bilko grabbed his bag off the rack, then barged his way down the aisle. The other passengers turned around and regarded him with polite hasn't-he-heard-of-queueing-horror. Bilko felt nothing but scorn for the pathetic specimens of humanity; if they didn't want to get off the bus in a hurry that was their fucking lookout, but he did. He stepped out onto the cobbled streets of Whitby's market square come bus station. The place was swarming with black-garbed hordes, all making their way to the bridge which crossed the tiny harbour to make their way up the steps to the festival. Booming guitars, white noise, and what sounded like sampled Gregorian chanting gusted over the crest of the hill opposite. Despite the bad atmospherics he could still recognise the sonic assault as 'Virgin Mary' by the Christian Cocksuckers. He sang along:

> '𝕮𝖍𝖗𝖎𝖘𝖙 𝖋𝖚𝖈𝖐𝖘 𝖍𝖎𝖘 𝖒𝖔𝖙𝖍𝖊𝖗 𝖚𝖕 𝖙𝖍𝖊 𝖆𝖗𝖘𝖊,
> 𝕿𝖍𝖊𝖓 𝖈𝖔𝖒𝖊𝖘 𝖎𝖓 𝖍𝖊𝖗 𝖒𝖔𝖚𝖙𝖍,
> 𝕬𝖓𝖉 𝖘𝖍𝖊 𝖋𝖚𝖈𝖐𝖎𝖓𝖌 𝖑𝖔𝖛𝖊𝖘 𝖎𝖙!'

One or two concerned looking Christians, their anoraks festooned with 'Festival of Light' badges, looked on in dismay, but the stupid do-gooders were hopelessly outnumbered and they knew better than to take this opportunity to spread the Word.

Bilko couldn't help but grin when he thought of his narrow escape from the Barrow guest house the night before. After tying Mrs B up and fucking her sensless he'd brutally murdered the daft old slag before writing obscene messages on the wall with her own blood. He'd barely had a chance to hide in the wardrobe when Mr B come bursting in. The daft old fucker hadn't been able to get it up in years, but the sight of his Mrs with her legs spread obviously turned the dirty old man on, and Bilko'd had no choice but to watch while he shagged the corpse. Minutes later the coppers had burst in, alerted by a worried guest, and they'd caught him with his pants down. In the intervening ten minutes between Mr B getting carted off for the benefit of society and the forensic mob arriving, Bilko had managed to leg it to the railway station. He'd signed in under a false name, so there were no danger of him being traced.

Now, as he trudged up the hundred or so steps, he were feeling strangely ennervated by the whole experience. The music were getting louder and louder, and it looked as if the festival was going to be a right good do.

Emerging onto the festival site, he recoiled in shock. Someone had beaten him to it. Some fucker had already torched the Abbey. Bilko couldn't fucking believe it. He'd been looking forward to putting the finishing touches to his devilish handiwork: completing the pentangle of fire; striking the last match that would imprint the mark of Satan across the length and breadth of England. His world was reeling, and the ruins of the abbey seemed to mock him, silhouetted as they were in the autumn sunshine. History weren't one of his strong points. He didn't know that Henry the Eighth had done his job for him four hundred years before.

He felt like the rug had been pulled out from under his feet. If someone else had torched the abbey, then how would he be able to complete his pact with the spirit dimension, and enlist their help in his ultimate goal of shagging Deb's brains out. He was snapped out of his reveried by a sudden shout:

'Bilko!'

*

Jeremiah Jones shuddered as he took to the stage. The satanic sounds of the Sisters of Mercy were booming from the next field, and it was time to summon the forces of goodness. He surveyed the ranks of Christian soldiers that were spread out en masse before him. Then stretched out his hands in a gesture that veered between supplication and subjugation. A hush fell over the crowd. They gazed up at Jeremiah Jones expectantly: he was quite an orator when he got really fired up.

Jones shuddered as he stepped up to the mic.

He smiled, but it died on his lips. Then before he could speak Jones shuddered again. He felt as if someone was walking across his grave. Then, without any warning, he felt the presence of... something evil. It was as if someone else had just walked into his body and... and... Jones was unable to resist the dark forces that he had unwittingly helped to summon when he'd sacrificed the Bishop of Derby on his own altar and which now filled the very heart of his being. A simple wooden sign shimmered into existence behind his head. On it was painted the legend: 'THOSE WHO DO NOT REMEMBER THE PAST ARE CONDEMNED TO REPEAT IT.' And though he couldn't have known it at the time, that was exactly what the man who had once been Jeremiah Jones was about to do.

The crowd murmured in confusion as the powerless preacher puppet staggered about. He felt his mouth open. It was as if he was little more than a ventriloquist's dummy. He could feel his mouth open to speak, but he had no idea what he was about to say. The rolling hills and the ruins of Whitby Abbey seemed to be fading in and out of focus, occasionally he seemed to be looking out of the windows of some crudely built wooden hall at the fields and jungle beyond. He tried to fight the ugly spirit that had invaded the heart of his very being, but could do little more than give a pathetic, strangled cough.

'How very much I've tried my best to give you a good life,' he said.

Or rather someone said, something said, with his voice.

Suddenly the ethereal wooden painted sign that shimmered behind him seemed to change. 'THOSE WHO DO NOT REMEMBER THE PAST ARE CONDEMNED TO REPEAT IT' it had once said. The last time that this sign had been gazed on by a vast number of Christian folk, it had been the last thing they saw. But that was then, and this was now, and while these good Christian folk gawped at the stage, the words 'DO' and 'NOT' just seemed to dissolve into thin air. Now the sign read "THOSE WHO REMEMBER THE PAST ARE CONDEMNED TO REPEAT IT'.

For it was no longer Jeremiah Jones that was standing before the massed ranks of Christians who had assembled for the Festival of Light Protest, he had been possessed by the spirit of Jim Jones, the late leader of the Peoples Temple; the man responsible for nine hundred odd people committing mass suicide in the South American jungle. And the spirit of Jim Jones didn't give a flying fuck about the Festival of Night in the next field. He didn't give a shit about the threat that Death Metal music may or may not represent to good Christian family values. What the suddenly re-corporalized Reverend Jim Jones was interested in was repeating the past, like the sign said. Repeating the past word for word.

'In spite of all that I've tried, a handful of people, with their lies, have made our lives impossible,' he went on, finding that the pale preacher man's larynx was effectively erasing his American accent, so that he sounded more like Tom Jones than Jim Jones.

'There's no way to distract ourselves from what's happened today.'

The ugly spirit was getting into his stride. The speech would last about half an hour, and by the time he finished he'd have taken all the gawping good folks with him.

'The betrayal of the century. Some have stolen children from mothers and are in pursuit right now to kill them, because they stole their children. I mean we are sitting here waiting on a powder keg and I don't think that is what we want to do with our babies. I don't think that is what we have in mind to do with our babies.

'It was said by the greatest of prophets from time immemorial: No man may take my life from me, I lay my life down. So just to sit here and wait for the catastrophe that's going to happen on that airplane, it's going to be a catastrophe, it almost happened here, it almost happened, the congressman was nearly killed here. But you can't steal peoples' children, you can't take peoples' children without expecting a violent reaction. And that's not unfamiliar to us either. If we only look at the old christians who weren't communists...'

Jeremiah Jones tried again, for a fleeting second, to regain control of his body, to fight the ugly spirit of the dead near-namesake who was now speaking through him, but was unable to do more than force the occasional cough;

'World opinion [cough] violence and violence [cough] force. But if we can't live in peace then let us die in peace. I've been so betrayed. I've been so terribly betrayed. We've tried, and [cough] what he said right this minute was that he said if it was only worth one day it was worthwhile [cough]. Right then, what's going to happen in a few minutes is that one of the people on that plane is gonna, is gonna shoot the pilot. I know that. I didn't plan it, but I know it's gonna happen. They're gonna shoot that pilot and down comes that plane into the jungle and we had better not have any of our children left when it's over cos they'll [cough] on us. The point is that this plane. I don't know how to say it. I've never lied to you. I never have lied to you. I know that's what's gonna happen. That's what he intends to do and he will do it. He'll do it. What it means, I've been loaded with many pressures seeing all these people behave so treasonous. It was just too much for me to put together, but I now know what he was telling me and it'll happen. If the plane gets into the air that is. So my opinion is that you be kind to children and you be kind to seniors and take the potion like they used to take in Ancient Greece. And step over quietly because we are not committing suicide, it's a revolutionary act. We can't go back. We won't lose it for long. We're not going back to tell more lies which means more congressmen. There's no way, there's no way we can survive. You'd be making a strike but we'd be striking against people that we don't want to strike against. We'd like to get the people that caused this stuff and if some people are prepared and know how to do that tell it to Timothy

Stone, but there's no plane. There's no plane. We can't catch the plane in time.'

A hush fell over the massed believers. They were hanging on the Jones puppet's every word.

'He's responsible for it,' the ugly spirit continued, 'He brought these people to us. He and Diana Myrtle. The people in San Francisco will not be idle over this. We do not take our death in vain you know.'

'Is it too late for Russia?' One of the congregation had stepped forward and shouted out a question, or rather something had spoken through the committed christian's mouth.

'Here's why it's too late for Russia. They killed. They started to kill. That's why it makes it too late for Russia. Otherwise I'd say yes sir you can bet your life, but it's too late. I can't control these people. They're out there. They've gone with the guns and it's too late. And once they've killed anybody, at least that's the way I want it. I just put my lot with you. If one of my people do something it's me. When they say I don't have to take the blame for this, well I don't, I don't live that way and if they deliver up and try to get the man that's it. And was mothers being lying on him and lying on him and trying to break up this family and they've all agreed to kill us by whatever means necessary. Do you think I'm going to let them? Not on your life. No you're not going. You're not going. You're not going. I can't live that way. I can not live that way. I've lived for all and I'll die for all. I've been living on hope for a long time. They make our lives worse than hell. And make the rest of us not accept us. They tell so many lies there in that truck. We are not in as far as any alternative. But to me death is not a fearful thing. It's living that's fearful. I have never never never seen anything like this before in my life. I have never seen people take the law, and do, and provoke us and try to purposely agitate the mothers of children. It's only, it's not, it's not worth living like this, worth living like this. There is one man there who blames, who blames Michael Stone for the murder of his mother, and he will stop that plane by any means necessary. There's no way you can fly a plane without a pilot. I haven't seen anybody yet that didn't die. And I like to choose my own kind of death. I'm tired of being [cough] to hell that what I'm tired of. Tired of it. So many peoples' life in my hands. I've been telling you to this day that without me life has no meaning. I'm the best friend you'll ever have. I have to pay. I'm standing with you people. You're part of me. I can't detach myself. I detach myself. No, no, no, no, no, no, no. I never detach myself from any of your troubles. I've always taken your troubles right on my shoulders. I'm not going to change that now. It's too late. I've been running to long. I'm not gonna change now.'

The crowd were silent as the spirit of Jim Jones continued to speak through the empty shell of the White Welshman.

*

Unaware of the ungodly goings on in the next field Bilko was concentrating solely on the pressing matter of not being suffocated by Tish's massive bulk. When he'd heard someone calling his name a few moments before he'd thought, for a second, that it might have been Deb. He'd turned round to greet the object of his devilish desires only to be confronted by the sight of Tish peeling off her clothes as she hurled herself bodily in his direction.

'Bilko!' she yelled. 'Fuckin Ell you look bloody gorgeous! Here I come you randy bastard!'

Suddenly he was pinned to the ground, and powerless to resist her urgent advances. Within seconds she had pulled his black Levis down around his knees and impaled herself on his blood-filled love bone.

'I wanna ride you to hell and back you fucker!' Tish yelled, as she ground her big arse down onto the unwitting object of her considerable affections.

Bilko was perplexed. This were all wrong. Everything were wrong. First the fucking Abbey and now this. It weren't Tish that fancied him it were Deb, the spirits had fucking told him so. He was powerless to resist, though, as the fat goth bird bucked and writhed above him like a banshee bitch on heat. Perplexed he might have been, but Bilko wasn't stupid. Tish were giving him the shag of his life, and realising that he might as well enjoy himself he grabbed hold of a tit with one hand and slid the other one down so's he could slip a finger up her hot arse. Tish reacted like a creature possessed, she sank her teeth into his neck and sucked till she could taste the bruise. By way of a reply, Bilko drove his thick, veiny cock deep into the hot, pulsating heart of her being.

What Bilko didn't realise as he felt the walls of the underworld closing in on him was that the blood-soaked tampon at the heart of his waxen devil doll were one of Tish's, the hair and the black lacey knickers too. The magic mannikin had worked alright, but it had worked on the wrong bird.

*

'What I'm talking about now is the dispensation of judgement. This is a revolutionary suicide council. I'm not talking about self, self-destruction. I'm talking about what, we have no other road. I will take your call, and I will put it to the Russians. And I can tell you the answer now because I am a prophet. Call the Russians and tell them, see if they'll take us.'

As Jim/Jeremiah droned on, half a dozen vats of fruit juice and a load of disposable cups shimmered into existence amongst the massed ranks of Christians who were spread out in front of the Festival of Light's stage. The dazed do-gooders, unable to shake off their love-thy-neighbour beliefs began to politely offer each other drinks and pass plastic beakers of the deadly refreshments amongst themselves.

'I tried to give you peace. I laid my life down practically. I practically died every day to give you peace. And you've still not had any peace. You look better than I've seen you in a long while, but it's still not the kind of peace that I wanted to give you. A person's a fool who continues to say that you're winning when you're losing. Win one, lose two. What? We win, we win when we go down. They don't have anybody else to hate. They've got nobody else to hate. Many will destroy themselves. I'm speaking not as the administrator but as a prophet today. I wouldn't talk so serious if I didn't know what I was talking about. By now the damage will be done. But I cannot separate myself from the pain of my people. I can't separate myself. If you think about it, we've walked together for too long. I saved them. I saved them. But I made my example. I made my expression. I made my manifestation and the world was ready. Not ready for me. Paul says I was a man born out of due season. I've been born out of due season just like we all are and the best testimony we can make is to leave this Goddam world. Everybody hold it. Hold it. Hold it. Lay down your burden and I'll lay down my burden down by the riverside. Shall we lay them down here, inside of Guyana, what's the difference? No man didn't take our lives right now, he hasn't taken them. But when they start shooting them out of the air they'll shoot some of our innocent babies. I'm not lying. It's fifty, there's fifty but they've gotta shoot me to get through to some of these people. I'm not letting them take your child. Would you let them take your child?'

*

After shooting his load into Tish's cunt, Bilko stood up and looked around. The festival were in full swing, and the scene which greeted him was a Bosch-like landscape of decadent and twisted desire; an empire of ungodly gratification. It was a Garden of Earthly Delights and he saw that it was good. The Australian Mayhem were playing, and low down in the mix he could hear that they were running a sample of the famous boot-leg recording of the Jonestown suicide speech. 'Funny,' Bilko thought to himself bemusedly. 'I never noticed that Jim Jones had a Welsh accent.'

It would soon be time for the headline act. Rumour had

it that the Dogs of Thor were gonna make some sort of grand
entrance in the next half hour or so.

*

'For months I've tried to keep this thing from happening. But I
now see that it's the will of a sovereign being that this happened
to us. And we lay down our lives in protest at what's being done.
And we lay down our lives to protest at what's been done. The
criminality of people. The cruelty of people who walked out of
here today. You know these people who walked out, most of
those white people. Most of those white people walked. I'm so
grateful for the ones that didn't. Those who knew who they are.
There's no point, there's no point to this. We have... we are born
before our time. They won't accept us and I don't think we
should sit here and take any more time for our children to be
endangered and if they come after our children and we give
them our children then our children will suffer forever.'

The Christian protestors began to scream and clutch
their throats, one by one they fell to the ground writhing and
frothing at the mouth as the strychnine took effect, but still the
drinks were politely passed from hand to hand.

'You have to be honest and if you say that you want to
run you'd have run with them 'cause anybody could have run
today. I know you are not a runner, and I'd... your life is precious
to me. It's as precious as John's and I don't... What I do I do
with weight and justice and judgement. And I have waited
against all evidence. Take ease, take ease, take ease, take ease,
take ease. Sit down, sit down, sit down. I tried so very, very hard.
They're trying over here to see what's in it. What's gonna
happen. Who is it? Get Dwyer out of here before something
happens to him. It's all over. It's all over. What a legacy, what a
legacy. Well the Red Brigade's the only ones that made any sense
anyway. They invaded our privacy. They invaded our home.
They followed us six thousand miles away. The Red Brigade
showed them justice: the Congressman's dead. Please get us

some medication. It's simple. There's no convulsions with it. It's just simple. Please get it before it's too late. The GDF will be here I tell you, get moving, get moving, get moving. Don't be afraid to die. If these people land here they'll torture our children. They'll torture some of our people here. They'll torture our seniors. We cannot have this. Are you gonna separate yourselves from whoever shot the congressman. I don't know who shot him. They speak of peace. They gotta right to how many are dead. Oh God. Almighty God. I don't know how in the world they are ever gonna write about us. It's too late. It's too late. The congressman is dead. The congress lady's dead. Many of our traitors are dead. They're still laying out there dead. I didn't but my people did. They're my people and they've been provoked too much. They've been provoked too much. What's happened here has been too... has been an act of provocation. Will you please hasten. Will you hasten with that medication. You don't know what you've done. I've tried. They saw it happen. Ran into the bush and dropped the machine guns. You've got to move. You've got to get that medication. You've got to move. Might be in about twenty minutes. You've got to step that way. It's the only way to step. The choice is not ours now, it's out of our hands. And I do hope that those battallions will stay where they belong and don't come up here. It's hard. It's hard only at first is it hard. It's hard only at first. Living, when you're looking at death, it only looks, living is much more difficult. Raising up every morning and not knowing what's going to be, the night brings, it's more difficult, it's much more difficult. Please for God's sake let's get on with it. We've lived as no other people have lived and loved. We've had as much of this world as you're gonna get. Let's just be done with it. Let's be done with the agony of it. It's far, far harder to have to watch you every day die slowly. And from the time you're a child to the time you get grey you're dying. This is a revolutionary suicide. It is not a self-destructive suicide. They'll pay for this. They brought this upon us and they'll pay for it. I leave that destiny for them. Who want to go with their child has a right to go with their child. I think it's humane. I want to go. I want to see you go through. They can take me. And they can do whatever they want to do. I want to see you go. I don't want to see you go through this hell no more. No more, no more, no more. We're trying. Everybody relax. The best thing you can do is relax and you will have no problem. You will have no problem with the thing if you just relax. It is not to be feared. It is not to be feared. It's a friend. As you're sitting there show your love for one another. Gone, let's get gone, let's get gone. Who are these? We have nothing we can do. We can't, we can't separate ourselves from our own people. For twenty years laying in some rotten old nursing home. Taken us through all these anguished years. They took us and they put us in chains and that's nothing. That's this, and that is there is no comparison to that to this. They've robbed us of our land and they've taken us and driven us and we tried to find ourselves. We've tried to find a new beginning but it's too late. You can't separate yourself from your brother and your sister. No way I'm gonna do it. I'm... I refuse. I don't know who fired the shot. I don't know who killed the congressman, but as far as I'm concerned I killed him. You understand what I'm saying? I killed him. He had no business coming. I told him not to come.'

*

As night fell, a strange and wonderful thing happened. Children in bedroom windows facing the sea stared out in wonder at the apparition which was looming out of the sea mist. It was like something off a film: a tall ship, fully rigged with flaming torches at the prow and stern was making her slow and stately progress into port. Any of the thousands who saw this vision would probably not have noticed that there was no wind, that the sails were hanging limply from the masts. Would not have thought to question the forces that propelled the ghostly galleon into harbour. Fishing boats were dwarfed by the scale of the vessel, conjuring images of Whitby's past. The glory days when

Captain Cook had set sail from this very harbour. The days when the biggest whaling fleets in Europe had once operated out of this village. The days when tall ships like this would have crowded into the harbour, when enormous carcasses would have been hacked up on the quaysides, when whores had promenaded and the town had rung to the noise of sailors roaring from tavern to tavern. The days when the brawling and the boasting would spill off the boats and onto the narrow streets.

A crowd of locals gathered on the dockside with a photographer from the North Yorkshire Echo who was keen to get a cover picture for next week's edition of the paper. From high on the stern a stout rope was tossed down by unseen hands and a local fisherman tied the vessel to the quay. A gang plank was slowly lowered from amidships to the sound of creaking ropes, before dropping down onto the cobblestones with a resounding crash.

The locals crowded around to see what cargo the stately ship had brought, what exotic visitors would deign to visit their sleepy seaside town in such elegant style.

It looked like a waterfall at first. A foaming torrent which poured over the gunwhales onto the gangway and frothed down towards the awestruck populace. Then with a joint scream of terror the sightseers scattered as the first of several thousand black rats cascaded onto the quaintly cobbled quayside. Some were not quick enough, and were tripped by the seething mass of rodents and quickly overcome by the fetid stench of pestilential decay which the vile creatures embodied. The throng of cursed creatures spread rapidly, running down every street and alley way of the scenic Yorkshire tourist attraction, some people dived into the water of the harbour, but even that seemed to be boiling with rats.

Within minutes there was no-one left on the dock. No-one to witness the disembarkation of the ships true cargo.

Vlad Vargstrom's coat hung loosely about his shoulders as, bearing a flaming torch aloft in one hand, he staggered unsteadily down the gangplank. Behind him were the other members of the Dogs of Thor. There were no excited onlookers to photograph their progress through the picturesque streets. No one saw them walking unsteadily up the hundred steps to the abbey. They walked in silence, stumbling occasionally on the uneven heritage paving but never once did they look down. They only faltered for a second or two before finding their balance and resuming their walk. Eyes fixed straight ahead, the strange ensemble made their way through the perimiter of the festival crowd. The motley collection of goths and satanists, of ageing bikers and black-garbed punks parted in silence to allow them through, all mesmerised by the strange procession. Then, in their wake, a murmer went up in the crowd.

'Eh! Iss the fuckin' Dogs, innit!'

'Iss the Dogs is that!'

'Aye, sound! Iss the fuckin' Dogs!'

As the ghostly goths made their way to the stage, the Australian Mayhem were finishing their set. As one the antipodean tribute merchants threw down their instruments and fled. It was as if they knew that these Scandinavian satanic songsters were somehow harbingers of ill.

Vargstrom threw his flaming torch into the crowd, setting fire to various black-garbed audience members, then picked up a guitar from the stage. It was still plugged in as he banged out an experimental, atonal chord. The other members of the band followed suit; picking up a bass, taking position behind keyboards or drums. The festival-goers looked on in a stunned silence which was punctuated only by the weird samples of people screaming and the recording of the Jonestown suicide speech that the Australian Mayhem had been running throughout the whole of their set.

Bilko was standing with Deb and Tish and that near the front. They were gobsmacked. What a fucking entrance. It were worth coming just to see this, never mind that they'd also seen brilliant sets by Succubus, the Hell Whores, the Christian Cock Suckers, Sisters, Bauhaus, Sepultura, 'the Neph'', The Rose of Avalanche, The Australian Whitehouse and The

Australian Mayhem. Them bands were all shit hot, but the Dogs were something else, and from the sound of it this was all brand new material.

  'Weird!' said Deb.
  'Wicked!' said Tish.
  'Sound!' said Bilko.

*

The screams of tens of thousands of dead and dying Christians rose and fell like leaves on the breeze, but still Jim/Jeremiah continued:

  'Die with respect. Die with a degree of dignity. Lay down your life with dignity, don't lay down with tears and agony. There's nothing to death. It's like Mack said, it's like stepping over into another plane. Don't, don't be this way. Stop this hysterics. This is not the way for people who are socialists or communists to die. No way for us to die. We must die with some dignity. We must die with some dignity. Before we had no choice but now we have some choice. And you think they're going to allow this to be done, and allow us to get away with this? You must be insane. It's only. It's something to put you to rest. Oh God. Mother, mother, mother, mother, mother please. Mother please, please, please, don't. Don't do this. Don't do this. Put down your life with this child but don't do this. Free at last. Keep your emotions down. Keep your emotions down The medication will not hurt you if you will keep your emotions down. If you will be quiet. It's never been done before, you say. It's been done by every tribe in history. Every tribe facing annihalation. All the Indians of the Amazon are doing it right now. They refuse to bring any babies into the world. They kill every child that comes into this world because they don't want to live in this kind of a world. Be patient, be patient. Death is... I tell you I don't care how many screams you hear. I don't care how many anguished cries. Death is a million times preferable to ten more days of this life. If you knew what was ahead of you, if you knew what was ahead of you you'd be glad to be stepping over tonight. Death, death, death is common to people. If you ask the Samoans they take death in their stride. Just be dignity, just be dignified. If you'll quit telling them they're dying. If you adults will stop some of this nonsense. Adults, adults, adults, I call on you to stop this nonsense. I call on you to quit exciting your children when all they're doing is going to quiet rest. I call on you to stop this now if you have any respect at all. Are we black, proud and socialist or what are we? Now stop this nonsense. Don't carry on this any more. You're exciting your children.

'No, no sorrow that it's all over. I'm glad it's over. Hurry, hurry my children hurry. Let us not fall in the hands of the enemy. Hurry my children hurry. There are seniors out here that I'm concerned about, hurry. I don't want to leave my seniors to this mess. Now, quickly, quickly, quickly, quickly, quickly... No more pain Al. No more pain, I said, Al. No more pain. Jim Cobb is laying on the airfield dead at this moment. Remember the moment. All of the moments that he, these are the people, the peddlers of hate. All we're doing is laying down our life. We're not letting them take our life, we're laying down our life. We're sick of their lies and we just want peace. All it is is taking a drink to take, to go to sleep. That's what death is, sleep. Whatever. I'm tired of it all. If you don't, don't fail to follow my advice you'll be sorry. You'll be sorry. If we do it then let they do it. Have trust in... You have to step across. We used to sing. This world, this world, it's not our home. Well it sure isn't. We were saying. It sure isn't. And we don't want to tell him. The only thing to tell him. Assure these kids. Can some people assure these children of the relaxation of stepping over to the next plane. We'll set an example for others. We set... One thousand people who've said we don't like the way the world is. Take our life from us. We laid it down. We got tired. We didn't commit suicide, we commited an act of revolutionary suicide protesting the conditions of an inhumane world.'

Jim/Jeremiah finished his speech just as the last of the

Christian protestors screamed out their agonized death throes. The pallid preacher, possessed no longer, only damned, stumbled and fell dead onto the stage then gazed with sightless pink eyes at the crowd of ten thousand purple-faced Christian corpses that blanketed the rolling hills in front of the stage.

On the other side of the ruined abbey, Vlad Vargstrom played another spastic chord and as he did so Bilko screamed out in agony. Tish and Deb and that recoiled in horror as he suddenly writhed on the floor next to them. The crowd quickly scattered as the well-groomed occultist writhed in agony. Bilko felt like the guy in every werewolf movie he'd ever seen. He felt like a million tortured spirits were occupying his body and trying to force his very muscles, bones and viscera into new and diabolical forms. Suddenly his frame was unable to cope with the vast and anguished multitudes that were attempting to occupy his very soul, and with a scream which was instantly silenced, Bilko exploded; his blood and viscera replaying in midair-microseconds the eternal anguish of the spirits. The fleeting forms of the agonized phantoms which Bilko had unwhittingly channeled onto this earthly plane were temporarily captured in a rain of his own blood and gristle, which seemed to be suspended in mid air above the heads of the terrified festival goers. Unearthly fizzogs seemed to move and blur before their eyes. Some who were too far away were 'oohing' and 'aahing' like it was some kind of fiendish firework display or part of the Dogs of Thor's light show or sommat. Then, as The Dogs bashed away like a bunch of retarded chimps on meth, the spirit-hordes of hell disappeared into the night time sky and the upturned faces of the festival audience were spattered in an even drizzle of Bilko-rain.

Vargstrom and Co. were falling apart too, quite literally. Hunks of skin were spattering the stage at the feet of the satanic songsters, till they were little more than skeletons that still plonked spastically at their instruments. But suddenly it were as if someone were playing the fucking film backwards, the gobbets of flesh and muscle and skin seemed to fly back up. It was as if some unseen hands were making plasticine models around the skeletal forms of the ex-Swedes which pranced comically on the stage with their musical instruments like the badly animated puppets in some Sunday afternoon Sinbad film. But there was nothing comical about the creatures that were being built there. And they bore little resemblance to the Nordic rockers whose bodies had become little more than the raw materials for some-one else's design. As the vile transformation continued, festival goers were plucked from the mosh pit, the screams dying in their throats as their bodies were smeared onto the hideously hybridized creatures, like so much modelling clay. Weird horned creatures sporting scaly wings, with tits and bollocks all over their bodies, covered in tongues and tentacles, and each staring at the world through many eyes, were standing on the stage in place of the Dogs of Thor, who quite literally no longer existed, even though some part of themselves had provided the maquettes on which these demons were modelled.

The monster that-had-been-Vargstrom stepped up to the mic.

Some of the more inebriated members of the audience cheered. Some acid casualties assumed that they and they alone had hallucinated the horrors of the past few minutes. Others simply stared in open mouthed terror.

An unearthly voice rang out through the gargantuan speaker systems:

'They say the Devil has all the best tunes,' it seemed to say. 'And they're right!'

With that the demonic-'drummer'-beast at the back of the stage kicked into a drum intro that was naggingly familiar. And as it did so, the ground before the stage seemed to open up. Tongues of fire shot high into the air, and the air was thick with the smell of burning flesh as hundreds of hapless festival goers fell into the fiery pit. But suddenly, from within the gates of Hades, a small figure emerged, surrounded by a chattering gaggle of malign-looking reptilian creatures unbounded by the laws of nature who swarmed out of Hell and spread their malign presences through the now-cursed audience, torturing and crucifying the terrified goths at will. Lucifer was rising, and Lucifer was a man. Middle-aged and with a receding hairline. He seemed untouched by the fiendish fires, and simply walked up onto the stage and took the mic.

Lucifer punched the air and shouted, 'Hello Whitby!' before launching into the first verse of 'Cumming in your hair tonight'!

'Eh!' Deb managed to scream through her terror as the former prog-rock drummer-and-replacement-front-man launched into a little dance routine. 'Iss him!!'

Then the Earth beneath her feet ceased to exist and she began to fall, and fall, and fall.

And scream, and scream, and scream.

For ever.

Afterword:

The plague spread rapidly from the North Yorkshire seaside town, killing millions in its path as it radiated across the country like the ripples from a stone tossed into some oily little puddle. A FatSat in geostationary orbit above the UK briefly flashed around the world the unmistakable image of a pentangle of fire which stretched across the land from Belfast and Pllwhelli in the west to Moffat in the north, Whitby in the east and Derby in the South, before it malfunctioned and fell out of orbit, causing a low level nuclear explosion during re-entry in the atmosphere above London. All the punters at the Festivals of Night and Light died and went to Hell where Lucifer entertains them for all eternity with his multiple award-winning back catalogue.

Meanwhile, the strange tall ship in Whitby harbour also finally divested it's real cargo. Not the plague rats, nor the Dogs of Thor, but angry and vengeful Norse gods who now shriek across the desolate landscape of a newly re-primitivized Europe like supernatural wolves and extinguish the few small and flickering flames of hope that remain.

THE END